KINGDOM OF SHADOWS

A Dark Retelling of Peter Pan

P.A. POWER

KINGDOM OF SHADOWS

A DARK RETELLING OF PETER PAN

P.A. POWER

Dedicated to Randy Power, Julie DeFisher, C.R. McCormack, Jenn, Celtic Blue2U, Izzy Krause, and so many more. Thank you for pushing me to write my stories.

PROLOGUE

On a cold, crisp autumn night, a mother lay sobbing in a hospital bed, her trembling hands clutching at her husband's sleeve. Mournful tears streaked her face as she wailed softly into the still air, her grief suffocatingly heavy. Beside her, a bassinet draped with a hand-knitted baby blue blanket sat eerily silent, its emptiness echoing the heartbreak in the room.

In the midwife's office nearby, the quiet hum of an old nurse did little to ease the somber atmosphere. A young nurse approached the older woman, her expression caught somewhere between indifference and discomfort. "What's the issue with the missus?" she asked, glancing briefly toward the room.

"She lost her baby," the older nurse replied, her tone clipped with reproach, as though the younger woman's detachment grated on her nerves.

The younger nurse blinked. "She had just gone into labor when I left this morning. How did she.. lose the baby?"

"When her bundle dropped, the cord was wrapped around his neck. He didn't make it."

"Oh, the poor soul," the young nurse murmured, her gaze softening. "We'll need to give her time, but they'll be here soon for the body."

Knocking lightly on the door, the young nurse entered with a hesitant smile. "Knock, knock. How are we holding up in here?"

The mother looked up, her tear-streaked face pale but resolute. "Oh, just a little longer, please. We haven't even named him yet."

"No, no, take your time," the nurse replied softly, her own voice faltering as the weight of the room pressed down on her.

A sudden cool breeze swept in, making her shiver. "Oh my, the weather must be turning. There's a storm rolling in. Let me close that draft; we wouldn't want our new mother catching a chill."

She hesitated, realizing the insensitivity in her words. "I'm sorry...I didn't mean—"

The mother shook her head weakly, a ghost of a smile flickering over her lips. "It's okay. Please, leave the window open. I'm waiting for the stars."

"The stars?" the nurse asked, her brow furrowing.

"I'm waiting for the second star to the right," the mother whispered, pointing toward a faint twinkle in the night sky.

The nurse hesitated but nodded. "As you wish. If you need anything, just call me." Adjusting the oil lamp on the wall, she retreated quietly, the door clicking softly behind her.

Silence settled over the room like a heavy blanket, as the mother's sobs grew quieter, her gaze transfixed on the open window. Suddenly, a faint shadow moved across the room and the flickering lamplight danced against the walls.

From the corner of the room, two shadows appeared. Then, a young boy stepped forward, his gaze falling on the bassinet. He hesitated as he saw the mother's disheveled hair clinging to her tear-streaked face, and her soft blue eyes, red and swollen from crying.

A single tear rolled down his cheek, and he said, "He's so tiny." Then, his voice began to tremble as he added, "He's...just a little baby."

The faint shadow fluttered close, a sparkle of wings shimmering faintly in the lamplight. "You know the rules," said the shadow. "None of us know when our time will come." Her voice was a gentle whisper, tinged with sadness.

The boy knelt beside the bassinet, his hand hovering uncertainly before he placed it gently on the baby's chest.

A soft, golden glow radiated from his touch, as he lifted the infant's soul into his arms. The baby's face lit up with a serene smile, his tiny hand reaching out as though to grasp the magic surrounding him.

"He's beautiful," the boy murmured, holding the baby close.

"You're right, he's precious," the small, shadow figure murmured, hovering near.

"What is this feeling?" The boy's voice cracked as he held the baby close.

"You're feeling her pain," said the shadow, her gaze shifting to the mother. "Her love and her loss."

"Why hers?" he asked, his brow furrowing.

His little companion sighed, covering the baby lightly with pixie dust as he yawned and sneezed. "That's just how it is. Come on, you know the way."

"Yes, after all these years. Second star to the right, straight on to—" His words faltered as the mother's voice broke the silence.

"Peter."

The boy froze, his eyes widening in surprise. "What?" he muttered, turning toward her.

The mother sat up slightly, her gaze fixed on him. "Peter. That's what I want to call him," she said, her voice trembling. "Hank, I want to name him Peter."

"Why Peter?" the man beside her asked, his tone wary.

"Do you remember the stories I use to tell you?" she whispered, pointing across the room.

"The stories?" Hank frowned, glancing around. "Wendy, what are you talking about?"

"About a boy I once knew."

"That's impossible."

9

The young boy stared at her, stunned. "Wendy?" he whispered, stepping closer, his shadow lengthening in the lamplight.

The woman's lips curved into a bittersweet smile. "Peter, it's been so long. You've grown up in your own way, haven't you?"

"Wendy, I think the loss has finally caught up to you—" Hank paused on his words as the feeling in the room changed.

The boy's expression softened. "Wendy, you...you remember me?" He stepped out of the shadows, and Hank's jaw dropped as he saw the unexpected visitor for the first time.

"How could I forget?" Wendy replied, tears streaming down her cheeks. "Please tell me you're here to take him."

"Where is he taking my boy?!" Hank growled out, his cheeks aflush.

"Take my sweet boy to a place where he'll never grow up; somewhere where he'll never be lonely."

The young boy hesitated, glancing at Hank, his bewildered expression shifting to one of quiet understanding. Wendy placed her hand over Hank's.

"He is not taking our boy anywhere," said Hank, clenching a fist.

The smaller figure then fluttered up to the boy's shoulder and said, "We only have until daybreak."

"Hank," Wendy said softly, "let me tell you a story. A story about a Kingdom of Shadows."

SICKNESS

The medical ward was a tomb of sound and silence, the raspy coughs of the sick punctuating the still air, mingling with the faint metallic clink of instruments being prepared in the corner. Gas lamps flickered weakly, casting long shadows over rows of pale, sweat-drenched children. The air reeked of antiseptic and despair, the scent clinging to every corner like a specter. The smell of Death himself clung to every living thing in the room.

Dr. Jacobson threw open the ward doors, fully revealing the scene to Dr. Andrews. "Dr. Andrews, do you really want to live in a society such as this?" His voice was weary but sharp, slicing through the oppressive quiet. "A society in which children suffer like this, and yet you do nothing about it?"

Dr. Andrews barely flinched. His face, cold and devoid of sympathy, twisted into a smirk. "That is enough, Dr. Jacobson. These poor, filthy bastards don't deserve the shot. I don't know why we waste our time and money trying to save the scum of the city. These children are the lowest of the low. I would not even call them a part of society at all. All the ones that matter to me are being cared for, good doctor."

Standing nearby, Sister Agnus let out a sharp gasp, her hands trembling as she clutched a clipboard to her chest. "Dr. Andrews, these are children! They are gifts from God."

Dr. Andrews snorted, brushing past her. "If God so loved them, Sister, He wouldn't have made them sick in the first place. And if He loved them now, He'd cure them or take His 'gifts' back. All I see is a room full of trash."

With that, he turned on his heel and strode away, his coat swishing behind him.

Sister Agnus' lip quivered as she whispered a prayer under her breath, while Dr. Jacobson placed a steadying hand on her shoulder.

"Come, Sister. The children need us more than he ever will."

They moved down the rows of cots, tending to each child as best they could with the limited supplies at their disposal. Then they stopped at one particular bed. A young man lay there, his auburn curls plastered to his forehead with sweat. His labored breaths came in shallow bursts, each one a struggle for survival.

"Here, child," Sister Agnus said softly, adjusting the damp cloth on his forehead. "Let's try to make you more comfortable."

Peter's eyelids fluttered open; his deep brown eyes clouded with fever. "Sister..." he rasped.

"Yes, child?"

"Am I... Am I going to die?"

Her lips parted, but no words came. She brought a hand to her mask, pressing it tightly against her face as tears began to fall. Her mask was already stained with the traces of countless prayers—prayers that, for weeks, had gone unanswered.

Peter managed a faint smile. "It's okay, Sister. I... I would've lived longer if it wasn't for this flu. And that joke of a doctor."

"Peter," she chided gently.

"Not Dr. Jacobson. He has heart." Peter's brows knitted together as a wave of pain racked his body. He groaned, squeezing her hand for comfort. "It's that other one. Sister I feel so alone."

Sister Agnus smoothed his hair back, her touch gentle as a mother's. "Sweet Peter," she whispered, "there was never a time when you were alone."

Peter's fevered gaze met hers, his lips trembling. "Sometimes it feels like I am, though. Alone in the dark."

She turned and pulled back the curtain beside his bed, revealing the full moon glowing brilliantly in the sky. "Look, child. See the moon? If you look closely, you'll see a face in it."

Peter squinted, blinking rapidly as if clearing his vision. After a moment, he nodded weakly. "I see it."

"Even when the moon hides behind the clouds, it's always there," she said softly. "Just like God. You may not always see Him, but He is here. And so am I."

Peter let out a long sigh, his grip on her hand tightening slightly. "One night, Sister, I'll close my eyes..."

"And when you open them," she said, her voice firm but kind, "you will be in the arms of our dear Lord."

"So... I'm going to die," he said, his tone more statement than question.

"Peter, my sweet boy," she said, her voice breaking, "I won't lie to you. We have known each other since you were found abandoned as a baby. I raised you at the orphanage, and when you got sick... I couldn't bear to see you go. That's why I came here, to care for you."

Peter's lips curled into a faint, bittersweet smile. "You always did have a soft spot for me."

"And I always will." Sister Agnus gently tipped a cup of water to Peter's lips, her steady hands betraying none of the tremors in her heart. "Here, sweet boy. Just a sip. That's it."

Peter drank weakly, his parched lips barely parting. "Thank you, Sister," he whispered, his voice little more than a breath.

She placed the cup on the small bedside table and stroked his damp curls. "Rest now, Peter. I'll be back shortly."

Peter gave her a faint nod, his eyelids fluttering closed. Sister Agnus stood, smoothing her habit, and walked toward Dr. Jacobson, who stood at the far end of the ward. He was bent over, his hands trembling as he gently lifted the still body of a young girl from her bed. Her frail form was wrapped in a white sheet, her hair spilling like golden threads over his arm. His eyes, red-rimmed and hollow, met Sister Agnus' as she approached.

"I'm not sure how much more I can take," he said, his voice cracking. He carried the girl toward a child-sized coffin on a nearby table. The coffin was plain and rough, made from cheap pine wood, but it was better than nothing.

"It may not be much, but it's better than a bedsheet and a hole in the ground. If God is to take them, let me send them properly home. With dignity."

Sister Agnus placed a hand on his arm, her touch a silent offering of strength. She reached down and picked up a small, handmade doll that had been tucked beneath the girl's blanket. The doll was simple, its face stitched with uneven eyes and a crooked smile, but it was clearly loved.

Agnus gently tucked it into the child's hands. "Here you go, Elizabeta. Don't worry. We'll take good care of Sammy."

Dr. Jacobson hesitated for a moment, then nodded. He arranged large, fragrant lilies on the girl's chest, their sweet scent overpowering the sour stench of sickness that clung to the ward. With a sigh, he placed the coffin lid over her, his hands trembling as he nailed it closed.

The sound of the hammer echoed in the silent ward; each strike a dirge for another life lost. When he was done, Dr. Jacobson hoisted the small coffin onto his shoulder and carried it outside. The night air was sharp and cold, a bitter contrast to the suffocating heat inside the ward.

A horse-drawn wagon waited in the street, its driver—a gaunt, wiry man—ringing a bell and calling out in a sing-song voice, "Bring out your dead! Bring out your dead!"

Dr. Jacobson approached the wagon, his jaw tightening as the driver turned toward him with a wide, wicked grin. "Oh no, not another poor soul," the man said mockingly. "Do you have payment for me to take this one?"

Dr. Jacobson's lips thinned. "You are the undertaker, one of the few in this town. A town that pays for your services. To demand that these poor families pay you to take care of their dead is deplorable."

The undertaker shrugged, his grin never faltering. "A man has to eat, good doctor. With the town's coffers running so low, I'm never guaranteed payment."

Dr. Jacobson's eyes darkened as he set the coffin in the wagon. "Is that why you've been counting your bodies twice? I know what game you're playing, but you won't with my children."

The undertaker's grin faltered for a moment before returning, though it now carried a hint of unease. "Careful with your accusations, Doctor. It wouldn't do to make enemies in a town like this."

Dr. Jacobson leaned closer, his voice low and full of steel. "If I catch you stealing from these families again, you won't need to worry about enemies, because I'll make sure you answer for it."

The undertaker said nothing, his grin slipping as he turned away to adjust the reins on his horse. Dr. Jacobson stepped back, watching as the wagon rattled off into the night, the bell tolling with each bump in the road.

Sister Agnus, who had followed him outside, stood silently by his side. She placed a hand on his arm again, this time holding on for longer. "You did right by her," she said softly. "By all of them."

Dr. Jacobson nodded, his shoulders slumping. "It doesn't feel like enough."

"It never does," Sister Agnus said, her voice thick with sorrow. "But it is all we can do."

JUNIOR REAPER

As Sister Agnus extinguished the last oil lamp in the ward, a soft, golden glow lingered, casting long shadows across the quiet room. Peter lay still in his bed, his frail chest rising and falling unevenly. "Angela," he murmured weakly, his voice barely audible.

Sister Agnus paused by the door, her heart aching. "Who is Angela, Peter?" she asked, turning back toward him.

Peter blinked slowly, struggling to focus. "She's a little girl. She came in a few days ago... she was scared. I promised her she wouldn't be alone."

Sister Agnus' throat tightened as she remembered the name. Angela had passed away early that morning. She hesitated, then approached the small wooden desk where the patient ledger rested. She flipped through the pages and confirmed what she already knew. Steeling herself, she returned to Peter's bedside.

"Angela is with God now," she whispered gently.

Peter's lips quivered, his wide eyes shining with unshed tears. He turned his face away, silent sobs shaking his fragile body. Sister Agnus wiped a tear from her own cheek, unable to bear the sight of him so broken. "Rest now, Peter," she said softly, her voice trembling. "I'll see you in the morning."

As she left, she paused at the doorway, looking back one last time before retreating into the dim corridor.

The hours dragged on, and Peter was alone in the silence of the ward. He stared at the ceiling, his mind wandering. His thoughts turned to the family he'd never had, the mother he had never known. He wondered if his life had mattered to anyone beyond Sister Agnus. The dreams of growing up—of running, playing, and laughing with friends—flickered in his mind like dying embers.

As his breathing slowed, the air in the room shifted. Shadows deepened and swirled, coalescing into a figure at the foot of his bed. Death was not the skeletal figure Peter had imagined, but a calm, almost soothing presence, cloaked in flowing darkness. His face was hidden, but his voice was low and resonant, filled with an unearthly gentleness.

"You've suffered much, Peter," Death said, stepping closer. "And yet, your soul remains pure and kind. I am sorry to see another child's name on my list tonight. Don't be scared. I just need you to come with me for a minute."

Peter's weak eyes widened. "Are you here to take me?"

Death nodded solemnly. "Yes. But I offer you a choice, Peter. You may cross over and find peace. Your mother is waiting for you on the other side."

"My mother?" Peter's voice cracked. "I never knew her. She died... didn't she? Is that why I was at the orphanage?"

Death inclined his head. "She died bringing you into this world. But she has watched over you from beyond. She waits for you, Peter."

Peter hesitated, the ache in his heart sharp and raw. "What's the other choice" he whispered.

Death regarded him for a long moment before speaking. "You can remain. Become a junior reaper. Guide the souls of children, so they won't be scared and alone as you were."

Peter's heart clenched at the thought of children, frightened and lost. "I don't want them to feel like that," he said, his voice firm despite his frailty. "I'll stay."

A faint smile played across Death's unseen lips. "You are brave, Peter. Braver than most. But you will not be alone." Reaching into his robes, Death clasped his hands together, and a fine dust rained down like a silvery mist. The air filled with the sound of soft, joyous laughter.

Peter's eyes widened as the mist coalesced into a tiny, shimmering figure. Wings like spun glass fluttered, tinkling like silver bells. The small fairy hovered before Peter, her glow casting a warm light over his face.

"What is this?" Peter asked in awe.

"A companion," Death said. "Born from the first laughter of a child. She will help you in your work and remind you of the joy that still exists, even in the darkest moments."

Peter reached out a trembling hand. The fairy landed on his palm, her wings vibrating with a soft hum. "What's her name?"

"She is yours to name," Death replied.

Peter smiled faintly. "Tinkerbell."

Death gestured to a door that materialized from the shadows. "Through there, is our first job of the night."

Before Peter could answer, a cold wind swirled through the room, and the scene around them melted into darkness. Peter felt a sudden tug, as though the world had yanked him forward. When the blackness dissipated, he and Tinkerbell stood beside a twisted wreckage—a Vanderbilt 1918 Simplex crushed beyond recognition.

The metallic smell of gasoline and blood hung in the air. The surrounding field was illuminated by moonlight, broken only by the distant glow of a train, its whistle fading into the night. Peter shivered; his newform untouched by the cold but weighed down by the sight before him.

"What happened here?" he asked, his voice trembling.

Death materialized beside him, his shadowed form steady amidst the chaos. "A father in a rush tried to race the train. Tragically, not everyone survived." He gestured toward the wreckage. "Paul is over there. Leave the girl—she is a survivor."

Peter turned to Death in alarm. "Where are you going?"

"To find the father," Death replied, his tone measured. "This task is yours, Peter. Tinkerbell knows what to do."

Peter watched as Death disappeared into the darkness, leaving him alone with Tinkerbell and the eerie scene before him. He swallowed hard and looked to the fairy, who darted toward the crumpled remains of the car.

Her light guided Peter through the wreckage to a young boy slumped beside a younger girl. The boy's breathing was shallow, his face twisted in pain. His arms were wrapped protectively around his sister, shielding her even in unconsciousness.

Peter crouched down, unsure of what to do. "Paul?" he called softly. The boy stirred, eyelids fluttering.

"I'm here," he murmured, his voice weak.

Peter hesitated, unsure of how to proceed. "What do I do?" he asked aloud.

Tinkerbell landed on his shoulder and tugged at his hair, pointing toward Paul. "Touch him," she instructed with a soft tinkling voice.

Peter reached out hesitantly and laid his hand on Paul's arm. A strange warmth surged through him as Paul's body stilled, and a second later, the boy's soul stood beside Peter, translucent and glowing faintly.

Paul blinked, looking down at his own body and then at Peter. "Hey, what's going on? I have to save my sister!" he exclaimed, his voice rising in panic.

Peter knelt beside him; his expression calm yet sympathetic. "Your sister will be fine," he assured him. "Help is on the way."

Paul hesitated, glancing back at the wreckage, his eyes filled with worry. Tinkerbell flew in front of him, her wand glimmering as she flicked it toward the sky. A radiant beam of light appeared, illuminating a staircase made of shimmering brilliance.

"No, I won't go. I can't go," Paul cried, as he ran to the nearby ledge, tucking himself under it and rocking back and forth. Peter slowly walked over and joined him under the ledge. Where they sat, they could see rocks tumbling past them into the ancient waters ahead.

"Why? Was I a bad boy? Am I being punished because I made Daddy run late?"

Peter took Paul by the hand. "No, sir. You were so good because you saved your sister. You protected her with your life. It's because of this that the boss sent me to take you to a special place."

"Heaven?" Paul whispered, the words barely making it past his lips.

"Yep, come on. Let's have ourselves an adventure." Peter stood up, extending his hand for Paul. As they both walked back, the staircase of lights shone bright; a glowing warmth radiating from it.

Paul stared at the staircase, awestruck. "Is that for me?" he whispered.

Peter nodded. "Tinkerbell says you should follow the light."

Paul hesitated, taking a step back. "I'm not scared," he said, more to himself than to Peter. "Momma always told us it's okay when God calls us home. She said the angels would guide us."

A soft smile broke across Peter's face. "Then you don't have to be afraid. Just climb the stairs, and the light will take you to her."

Paul turned toward the staircase as a faint whisper drifted down. His eyes widened, and he broke into a run. "Momma!" he cried, his small frame disappearing into the golden glow.

Peter stood still, watching the boy ascend until the light faded and the stairs dissolved into the night. He sighed deeply, a strange mix of sorrow and peace filling his chest.

Tinkerbell fluttered to his side, her tiny hand patting his cheek in reassurance.

Then, Death reappeared, his shadowed form solid and imposing. "You did well, Peter," he said, his voice warm with approval. "The boy is with his mother now."

Peter turned to Death, his curiosity overcoming his sadness. "Paul said his mother died."

"Yes, she died of the Spanish flu." Death looked at his book before returning it to his robes.

"Why couldn't she stay with him when she passed?" Peter looked up inquisitively.

Death paused for a moment, considering his words. "Sometimes, the living cling to those who have gone, and the dead cannot move forward. But when the time comes, souls find each other again in the light."

Peter nodded, his gaze dropping to the ground. "What happens to the girl? His sister? You said you came for their father."

"She will live," Death replied. "Her journey is not yet over. That is all I can say, boy."

As Peter processed this, Death handed him an aged, leather-bound map. Peter unfolded it, revealing a detailed drawing of a fantastical island surrounded by unending sea.

"What's this?" Peter asked, frowning.

"A map," Death replied simply.

"I can see that," Peter said, rolling his eyes. "What's it for?"

Death's unseen smile was almost tangible. "It is to Neverland. A place between realms, where you will find sanctuary and solace between your tasks."

Peter studied the map, the details blurring and reshaping as he looked. "Why is it called Neverland?"

"Come, and you will see." Death stretched out his hand.

Peter glanced at Tinkerbell, who nodded eagerly. Then, with a deep breath, he said, "I'm ready."

Death raised his hand, and the world around them dissolved into shimmering light, pulling Peter and Tinkerbell into the start of their next journey.

"We're here Peter. This place is called Neverland, because here, you will never grow old, and you will never be alone," Death said. "It will take on the shape of your desires, Peter. A reflection of what you imagine a child's safe haven should be."

They looked out upon a vast landscape that was strangely empty, like a blank slate. Then, as if pulled from the depths of Peter's heart, a vibrant world began to bloom. Rolling hills, towering trees, and sparkling rivers filled the void. The sky glowed with a perpetual twilight, and laughter echoed faintly in the distance.

"Peter. This is your new home."

Death stood beside Peter, watching as he absorbed the beauty of the land. "This is Neverland. It will be your sanctuary between tasks. A place shaped by your memories and emotions; a haven for young souls who are not ready to cross. Here, you will never grow old, and you will never be alone."

Peter turned to Death, his eyes shining with wonder. "So, it's for the children?"

Death nodded. "And for you, Peter. To guide them—and to heal yourself. There is a place you must promise me you will never go Peter. Promise me you will use the map it will show you." Death paused his words lost in the wind as Peter was already off exploring Neverland.

DAWN'S TWISTED LIGHT

Dr. Anderson stood at his desk, a glass of brandy swirling lazily in his hand, the amber liquid catching the dim light of his office lamp. A sinister smile curled his lips as he muttered, "People trust me with their children's lives. They really shouldn't."

His gaze drifted toward the shadowed corner of the room, where a faint flicker from the fireplace cast dancing shapes on the wall. He was lost in thought until a sharp knock at the door jolted him back to reality.

"Dr. Anderson," a woman's voice called softly through the heavy oak door.

His expression twisted with irritation. "Can a man not get a moment's peace in this place?" he barked, stalking to the door. Fire blazed in his eyes as he threw it open. "Who dares knock on my office door at this hour?" His tone was as cold and hard as steel.

The young woman on the other side flinched slightly but stood her ground, her voice trembling. "Forgive me, sir, but it's one of the children."

Dr. Anderson's gaze flicked over her, lingering on her soft, apple- cheeked face, and the graceful curves that made his breath hitch for a fleeting moment. A faint shiver passed through his guarded heart, but he quickly masked it with a scowl.

"What child demands my attention at this ungodly hour?" he barked, his voice softening only a fraction, though it still carried his usual authority.

"It's the Rose Ward, sir," she replied quickly, her voice steadying as she turned and briskly led the way back down the dimly-lit corridor. Clipboard in hand, the candy striper's determined strides contrasted with the unease lingering in her eyes.

Dr. Anderson followed, grumbling under his breath as his shoes clicked against the tiled floor. The Rose Ward was for those families who could afford his personal care—or at least the illusion of it. As he approached the unit, he donned his protective equipment with deliberate precision, ensuring the virus wouldn't touch him. After all, he was the one who had introduced it.

Entering the ward, he was met with a surprising sight. Dr. Jacobson stood near a bouquet of fresh lilies, carefully arranging the flowers in a vase. "Dr. Jacobson," Anderson greeted curtly, his tone sharp. "Why are you in my ward? I thought I made it clear that your kind of filth isn't welcome here."

Dr. Jacobson tilted his head "Your ward?"

Dr. Anderson sneered. "MY ward? These families pay me good money to ensure their children receive the best care. What could a doctor of your caliber possibly contribute to this place?"

"The lilies, for one thing," Dr. Jacobson replied evenly, brushing past Anderson to adjust the flowers. "Their scent—unlike your attitude—helps mask the stench of death."

Dr. Anderson scoffed and turned his attention to the candy striper and nurses bustling around the ward. "Keep them busy, Jacobson. I've no time for your moral posturing." He stormed out, muttering about wasted efforts and inferior staff.

Jacobson, left alone, shook his head and sighed. As he exited the Rose Ward, he made his way to the nearly forgotten wing of the hospital—a place where the oil lamps held less oil, the halls were cleaned less often, and the smell of despair lingered like an unwelcome guest.

Supplies were scarce, and funding nonexistent, but this was where the real work was done. Here, he and Sister Agnus bore the weight of their responsibilities with quiet determination.

"Sister Agnus," Jacobson began as he approached the devout nun, her hands busy tending to a sick child. "Forgive my earlier outburst. My heart is heavy, and my mouth betrays me."

She paused, offering him a kind smile. "Easy, child. God knows the burdens you carry. He forgives you, as do I." Her fingers resumed their work as she whispered prayers under her breath, her voice a soothing balm against the chaos around her.

Their quiet moment was shattered when the doors flew open. Dr. Anderson entered, his mask tightly fitted, his eyes narrowing as he scanned the room. "You know, Jacobson," he sneered, "I had hoped I'd never see this place again, but you just had to stick in my craw. How dare you scare my staff with your talk of death?"

Jacobson leaned against the wall; pity evident in his gaze. "This is my world, Anderson. The light here is different, the smells sharper. You see filth and decay, but I see hope—fragile though it may be."

Anderson's lips curled in a mocking smile. "Hope? These are husks of humanity. You may wallow in this filth, but I am a superior doctor. My skill rivals the miracles your precious God supposedly performs."

"Blasphemy," Jacobson muttered, shaking his head. "Say what you will, Anderson, but when your wards—the ones you value so highly for their money—succumb to this virus, what then? What will you tell their grieving families?"

Anderson's smile widened. "Simple. If they're wealthy, I'll blame incompetent nurses or hapless candy stripers. If they're penniless, I'll send them here. You seem all too happy to take in the refuse of this hospital."

Jacobson's expression hardened as he pulled a folded paper from his jacket. "I've been looking into you, Anderson."

Anderson's smug demeanor faltered. "Watch your tongue, Jacobson. You don't know who you're dealing with."

"Don't I?" Jacobson unfolded the paper, holding it up. "You've done a lot of traveling, haven't you? Every year, a different hospital, a different ward. And yet..."

Anderson snatched the paper from Jacobson's hands, his face darkening. "I'm a traveling doctor. They pay for the best care, and I deliver. It's called privilege; something you wouldn't understand."

Jacobson didn't flinch. "Maybe. Or maybe it's something darker."

Anderson's eyes burned with barely contained fury as he turned on his heel and stormed out of the ward. His muttered words echoed faintly in the empty corridor.

"Each year, one trip. Just one. No one can link them to me. The government pays me to...cleanse. To eradicate the unworthy. And no sanctimonious fool like Jacobson will ruin me."

GUIDING LIGHT

The quiet hum of the ward was broken only by the raspy breathing of children clinging to life. Peter stood in the shadows, Tinkerbell perched on his shoulder, her wings glowing faintly. Sister Agnus knelt beside a small bed, her hand gently stroking the hair of a frail girl. The child's breaths came in short, laborious gasps, yet her pale lips curved into a serene smile as Sister Agnus whispered to her softly.

"Lord, I pray that You send a guide for her sweet soul. Do not let her suffer. We have done all we can," she murmured, her voice heavy with exhaustion and tinged with an ache only Peter could truly understand. She paused to wipe her brow, her hands trembling slightly. "Sweetheart, before you depart, if you see my boy tell him I love him."

As she walked away, a subtle cough escaped her lips—a harbinger of the flu's relentless grip—but she straightened herself and continued down the row of beds, offering what little comfort she could.

Peter stepped out of the shadows; his movements soundless as he approached the small bed. The little girl stirred, coughing lightly before giggling.

"She's a kind lady," the girl said, her voice weak but bright. "She told us all about you."

Peter's brow furrowed, and he sat down beside her. "About me?"

"She said when our time comes God sends us all an Angel to carry us home."

Peter exchanged a glance with Tinkerbell, who fluffed to the girl's pillow, her light casting a soft glow over the child's pale face.

"How would she…" Peter paused looking down at the girl.

"She buried him, you know," the girl continued, her blind gray eyes staring straight ahead. "Up on the hill. Used all her savings to buy a grave with an angel sitting on it. Crying, just like her."

"I'll have to see that later," Peter muttered, his voice catching. The girl turned her head toward the sound of his voice.

"Can I go too?"

Peter hesitated, his hand hovering over hers. "Tink," he whispered, leaning closer. "She's blind."

"I know," the girl answered before Tinkerbell could chastise Peter. "The fever took my sight first. Then the flu set in, and it's been downhill since. But I feel okay with you here. What's her name?" She pointed directly at Tinkerbell, her aim startlingly precise.

Tinkerbell twirled in the air, her wings shimmering as she landed softly on Peter's shoulder.

Peter smiled, taking the girl's frail hand in his. "Her name is Tinkerbell. Come with us, Olivia."

"How'd you know my name?" the girl asked, her lips forming a tiny pout.

"I know a lot of things," Peter teased gently. He stood, and as he did, the child's soul rose effortlessly from her body to stand beside him.

"I can see again!" she squealed, twirling in place.

Peter winced dramatically, sticking a finger in his ear. "Well, I can hear just fine, thanks."

"Oops, sorry," she said, giggling.

"It's okay. Come on, Olivia. There's something I want to show you."

Tinkerbell fluttered ahead, and in the blink of an eye, they were standing on a hill overlooking the cemetery. Peter's gaze landed on a gravestone adorned with a crying angel—a small, marble boy.

"That's no angel," Peter muttered.

"Sure it is," Olivia countered, beaming. "Sister Agnus said he just hasn't earned his wings yet."

Peter's throat tightened as he knelt to read the name etched into the stone: Peter Pan. His fingers traced his name, causing him to pause briefly as a tear escaped his eye.

"You're Peter!" Olivia gasped.

"Guilty," he said, offering a faint smile.

"Why aren't you in Heaven?"

Peter sighed, brushing a hand through his hair. "I've got a job to do, that's all."

Olivia tilted her head. "So, do I have to go to Heaven right now?"

"Not if you don't want to," Peter replied, gesturing to the Heavens. "You can stay in Neverland for a while if you'd rather."

"What's Neverland?"

"A place where you'll never feel alone. A place for kids like you. A place for kids like me."

Her eyes lit up. "Can I go?"

Peter glanced at Tinkerbell, who waved her wand. A golden doorway appeared, revealing faint stairs stretching into a starry sky.

"Your destiny awaits," Peter said softly. "It seems your soul is at peace, and you're ready for Heaven."

Olivia hesitated, staring at the dim glow of the stairs. "They're not very bright," she whispered, as her shadow started to grow larger and darker.

Peter knelt beside her. "They will be. You just need faith, trust, and..." He blew a pinch of pixie dust over her, and the stairs began to shine brilliantly, causing her shadow to shrink back away from the light.

Olivia giggled as she stepped forward, pausing only to glance back. "Peter, thank you."

"Go on, kid," he said, his voice thick with emotion.

As the door closed behind her, the hill plunged into silence, and Death appeared beside Peter, his presence both foreboding and comforting.

"Peter?"

"Death," Peter replied, his voice weary. "She told me about Sister Agnus. How she buried me."

Death placed a firm hand on Peter's shoulder. "This place is sacred, Peter, but don't let it consume you. There's more suffering out there—children who aren't as lucky as you were. Many are buried in pits, forgotten and nameless. Your role is to guide them; to ensure they find light."

Peter nodded, swallowing hard. "I'll do my best."

"I know you will," Death said softly, vanishing into the night.

Peter stood there for a moment longer, gazing at the stars. "Come on, Tink," he murmured. "We've got work to do."

As the wind carried his words, Peter turned away, his heart heavy with purpose—and with the first seeds of doubt. In but a few blinks of an eye they were gone to their next calling.

Peter sat perched on the edge of a dilapidated windowsill, the muffled giggles of two boys filtering through the cold, moonlit air. He peered into the room, his sharp eyes catching sight of the twins huddled together under a threadbare blanket. Their identical faces were pale but full of mischief, their eyes glinting even in the dim light.

"Are you sure it's not your turn, Timmy?" one whispered, his voice hoarse but spirited.

"No, Tommy, you're cheating again!" came the defiant reply, though the boy's grin betrayed the seriousness of his accusation.

Peter felt his chest ache, a bittersweet mixture of longing and sadness curling inside him. "They're just like I was..." He glanced at Tinkerbell, perched on his shoulder with her tiny arms crossed, her glow flickering impatiently.

"They're not ready to leave," Peter murmured.

Tinkerbell's tinkling voice filled his ear. "You know the rules, Peter. They have to cross over there is nothing left for them here."

Peter hesitated before stepping through the shadowy veil that concealed him, his boots landing silently on the creaky wooden floor. The twins froze, wide-eyed, as his shadow stretched ominously across their blanket.

"Relax," Peter said with a crooked smile, crouching to meet their gaze. "I'm not here to scare you."

Timmy tilted his head. "Then who are you?"

Peter sat cross-legged on the floor, his face softening. "I'm Peter. I help kids like you find someplace better."

Tommy squinted, suspicious. "Better than here?"

Peter chuckled. "Yeah, much better than here. No doctors, no sickness, no scary nights. Just..fun."

Timmy's face brightened. "Like games? Hide and seek?"

"And sword fights?" Tommy added.

Peter's grin grew. "Exactly like that."

Tinkerbell huffed, flicking a tiny spark of light in their direction. "Peter!" she whispered sharply in his ear.

Peter ignored her, watching the boy's once dull and lifeless face, sparkle and shine. "But here's the thing," Peter continued, leaning closer, his voice dipping into a conspiratorial whisper. "I don't usually bring kids back with me. It's...special. Just for the brave ones."

The twins' eyes widened in unison. "We're brave!" they chorused. Peter glanced at Tinkerbell, who sighed but finally flitted to his side.

"Fine," she said, her glow softening. "Faith, trust, and a pinch of pixie dust. But they'll need to think happy thoughts, or it won't work."

"What's a happy thought?" Timmy asked, frowning.

"Something that fills you with light," Peter explained. "Like...your favorite memory. Something that makes you laugh or feel safe."

The twins exchanged a glance, then closed their eyes. Timmy spoke first. "I'm thinking of the time we built a fort under the bed and pretended to be pirates."

"And I'm thinking of when we snuck into the kitchen and ate all mommy's strawberry jam," Tommy added, snickering.

"Perfect," Peter said, standing and stretching his arms out. "Now hold on tight."

The boys grabbed his hands, and Tinkerbell flew above them, sprinkling golden dust that shimmered like starlight.

"Now, think of your happy thoughts," Peter instructed, his voice light but steady. "Let them lift you up. We're off to the second star to the right, straight on till morning!"

The room dissolved into a swirl of light and laughter. The twins gasped as they floated, the cold, dreary room replaced by endless stars. Peter led the way, his blue coat billowing behind him, his laugh echoing through the night.

Tinkerbell flew circles around the twins, her light leaving trails of gold as they soared through the night sky. Ahead, Neverland came into view—a sprawling island of lush jungles, sparkling waters, and endless adventures.

"We're here," Peter announced, landing gracefully on the soft grass.

The twins tumbled down, laughing as they rolled into the warmth of Neverland's embrace.

Tommy and Timmy looked around in awe. "This is amazing!"

Peter smiled, his loneliness momentarily forgotten. "Welcome to Neverland," he said. "You're going to love it here."

But as Tinkerbell watched from her perch on a nearby branch, her glow dimmed with unease. "This isn't how it's supposed to go, Peter."

"Come on Tink, they were not ready, and to be honest I am a little lonely," Peter pouted.

"Fine, don't say I didn't warn you." With that, Tinkerbell fluttered to her favorite tree and crawled into the hole where her house sat.

CROW

Peter flew up high above Tinkerbell and the boys and let out a loud rooster's crow, "Cock-a-Doodle-doo!" This sent the boys into a fit of laughter, seeing Peter high in the sky with his hands on his hips.

"Boys, don't mind Tink; she's more of one to follow the rules," Peter teased, making a mockingly stern face that sent the twins into more belly- filled giggles.

"So, what now that we're here? You call this place Neverland?" Tommy mused.

"Yes," Peter replied with a grin. The moment Peter clasped each twin's hand, an electrifying surge of energy rippled through them. With a mischievous glint in his eye, he asked, "Ready to fly?"

The twins nodded hesitantly.

"Just think happy thoughts," Peter encouraged. "And don't look down…unless you want to!"

With that, he launched them all into the sky. Timmy let out a startled yelp, while Tommy's laughter rang out like wind chimes. They soared higher, the lush expanse of Neverland unfolding beneath them. A mosaic of emerald forests, sparkling blue rivers, and golden beaches stretched as far as their eyes could see. The twins were in awe.

"This is incredible!" Tommy exclaimed; his voice nearly lost in the wind.

Peter chuckled. "Wait until you see what's hidden in those trees. Neverland isn't just beautiful; it's alive."

He guided them in a graceful arc over the island, pointing out landmarks.

"That's Mermaid Lagoon," he said, gesturing toward a shimmering cove, where figures with glistening tails lounged on rocks, their laughter echoing faintly. "And over there is Skull Rock. Not the friendliest place, so we'll keep our distance."

Skull Rock rose like a jagged scar on the horizon, its sharp edges and ominous silhouette cutting through the gray mists that clung to the Neversea. The water below churned violently, as if the ocean itself rejected the presence of the sinister landmark. Peter's heart quickened as he caught sight of it in the distance, its shadow seeming to stretch unnaturally far, as though reaching for the unwary.

"Why does everyone avoid Skull Rock?" Tommy asked, his voice steady but his curiosity laced with unease.

Peter shifted uncomfortably. "It's not just a place—it's like a wound," he croaked, his eyes narrowing. "No light touches it. No sound escapes it, save for the screams of those who venture too close. Even the bravest of us doesn't linger."

Peter glanced down at the swirling waters below, where the occasional glimmer of shattered moonlight appeared and disappeared. "What happens if someone goes there?" Tommy pressed.

Peter shook, as if to shake off an unseen chill. "The stories say it's a gate between worlds. A maw that devours. The unworthy souls who stray too close are stripped of their form, their essence drawn into the abyss. They don't return." His voice dropped lower, until it was almost a whisper. "And if they do, they're not the same."

As they flew closer, Peter noticed figures darting across the waters surrounding the Rock. At first, he thought they were ordinary pirates, their tattered sails flapping in the gale, but something about them felt off. Their movements were too fluid, their forms too shadowy. Then he saw their faces— or rather, the void where their faces should have been.

"Reapers," Peter muttered. "Those aren't pirates, Tommy. I think that's what's left of my kind when we forget our purpose."

Peter's stomach churned as he watched the figures—grinning skulls where their faces should have been, cloaked in ragged shadows. Their ships creaked unnaturally, black mist spilling from their hulls as they circled Skull Rock in a ghostly dance.

"Why do they look like that?" Timmy asked, his voice barely audible over the howling wind.

"I think they chose to wear the guise of pirates," Peter explained. "It's the shape of their torment—a reflection of who they were or what they once feared most. They're lost souls, Timmy, trapped in the liminal space between duty and oblivion. The Rock calls to them, and they can't resist."

Peter shivered as he tore his gaze away from the spectral ships. The air around Skull Rock felt heavier now, pressing down on him like an invisible weight. "Let's keep going," he said firmly, gripping his dagger tighter.

As they began to move away from the Rock, Peter instructed, "Never let curiosity guide you toward that place. It hungers for wanderers like us."

As they ascended higher, Peter cast one last glance back at the foreboding sight. The skeletal forms aboard their spectral ships seemed to pause, as if sensing his gaze. Their eyeless sockets burned with an eerie light, and Peter quickly turned away, focusing on the horizon. Even from a distance, the chill of Skull Rock lingered, a reminder that some places in Neverland were best left untouched.

"That is one of the places I will warn you do not go near, the other is marked on my map." Peter pulled the map from his pocket showing it to them.

"All it says is forbidden in a blue heart." Tommy whispered.

"Hey I don't make the rules I just follow them, well most of the time." Peter half-heartedly let out a soft chuckle.

The further from Skull Rock they flew, the safer they all started to feel. Suddenly, the twins' eyes widened as they passed over a dense jungle, its treetops whispering secrets. Peter slowed, hovering near a towering banyan tree with roots that seemed to hold up the world.

"This," he announced, "is where you'll build our fort. Tommy looked skeptical.

"How are we supposed to do that? We don't have tools or...anything."

Peter's grin widened. "In Neverland, all you need is your imagination."

He set them gently on a thick branch that jutted out like a natural balcony. The twins exchanged curious glances before closing their eyes, focusing on their dreams.

"What kind of fort do you want?" Peter asked, his voice soft, almost reverent.

"A treehouse," Tommy whispered, his voice trembling with excitement. "With a spiral staircase wrapping around the trunk, a rope bridge, and...oh! A swing made from vines."

Timmy added, "And turrets! It needs to feel like a castle...but also a pirate ship!"

As they spoke, the air shimmered around them. The tree began to shift and grow, responding to their words. Thick vines wove themselves into sturdy ropes, forming the bridge Tommy had imagined. Branches twisted and extended, crafting spiral staircases, lookout turrets, and a crow's nest with a perfect view of the island. The trunk hollowed slightly, revealing cozy rooms with walls adorned by glowing mushrooms and twinkling firefly lights.

When the twins opened their eyes, they gasped. Their dream fort stood before them, a living testament to their imagination.

"Is this real?" Tommy asked, stepping cautiously onto the rope bridge.

Peter laughed. "As real as Neverland itself. Go on, explore it."

The twins darted through their creation, climbing, swinging, and marveling at every detail. Timmy leaned over the edge of a turret; his cheeks flushed with excitement. "This is the best place ever! We're never leaving!"

Peter hovered nearby, his expression softening. "That's the magic of Neverland," he said quietly. "It's a piece of you, made real."

As the sun got lower, casting a golden glow over the island, the twins curled up in their new fort, exhausted but exhilarated. Peter perched on a branch nearby, watching them with a mixture of pride and something deeper—a longing he couldn't quite name. For now, they were safe, happy, and home.

And in Neverland, that was all that mattered.

SKULLS & CROSSBONES

The sea thundered against the hull of the ghostly ship, the *Jolly Roger*, its jagged sails black as the abyss. A motley crew of spectral pirates moved with eerie precision, their hollow eyes glinting like stolen stars in the dim glow of the lanterns swinging overhead.

The salty air was heavy with tension as the captain stood at the helm, towering over his men like a storm given flesh. His coat was tattered but regal, with gold trim that caught the faint light. His hat, adorned with a plume as white as bone, cast a long shadow over his skeletal grin.

"Captain, did you see?" Smitty, a wiry man with a twitch in his left eye and a voice like gravel, pointed toward the horizon, where spectral lights shimmered faintly.

"Aye, Smitty. Three young souls adrift in the veil," the captain growled, his voice as deep as the ocean's trenches. "But only two carry a bounty worth our trouble. The third..he's different. A reaper's apprentice, no doubt. Yet untested, unworthy of the scythe he bears."

Smitty scratched his unshaven chin nervously. "Death's got himself a new pet, eh? Captain, you know he'll come down hard on us if we rob from his ranks."

The captain's hollow laughter filled the air, chilling the crew to their core. "Ah, Smitty. Even Death can't defy the laws that bind us all. A soul must cross over in its time. If this young reaper fails in his duty, we'll be there to claim what's ours. The lost, the defiant, the broken—they all come to us eventually."

Smitty's lips curled into a crooked smile. "It's been a long while since we've taken children, Captain. Pure souls like theirs..they're worth more than double, if I recall."

41

The captain's skeletal fingers drummed on the helm. "More than double, my dear Smitty. They're treasures beyond measure. Let this young reaper come and play his part. One day, when he's not looking, we'll swoop in and claim the lot. His failures will be our bounty." He threw his head back and let loose a vile laugh that echoed across the waves like a death knell.

"Captain, we're ready," one of the crew croaked, bowing low. The man's gaunt frame cast a grotesque shadow in the lantern light, his eyes glinting with malice.

The captain turned sharply, his hollow sockets blazing with spectral fire. "Take us out, Smitty. We've a storm to ride and lost souls to plunder. Let no mortal tether nor reaper's scythe stay our course."

"Captain," Smitty whispered, his voice trembling now. "Skull Rock...it's watching us."

The captain turned, his fiery gaze locking onto the distant Rock. The glowing sockets seemed to flare brighter, as if alive with warning. He spat over the side of the ship. "Let it watch. We answer to no one, not even the cursed rocks of the sea. Onward, lads! The storm's fury is our ally, and the lost souls of the veil are our prey."

The *Jolly Roger* groaned as it pulled away from Skull Rock, a towering formation that loomed over the sea like a watchful sentinel. Its cavernous eye sockets emitted an eerie glow, bathing the ship in a sickly green light as if bidding farewell. The waters churned violently, as if the sea itself sought to expel the unnatural vessel.

As the ship plunged into open waters, the rough seas transformed into a boiling tempest. Lightning flashed, illuminating the skeletal figurehead of the *Jolly Roger* that seemed to leer at the ocean ahead.

The crew moved like wraiths, tying ropes and securing the sails with inhuman speed and efficiency. The captain stood firm, his gaze fixed on the horizon, where the storm brewed darkest.

"Captain," Smitty called, his voice barely audible over the howling wind. "The souls...can you feel them?"

The captain's grin widened, his teeth glinting like blades. "Aye, Smitty. They call to us, desperate and afraid. Their cries sing sweeter than the sirens' song. We'll skim the ocean floor if we must, but those souls will be ours."

The ship's bow dipped below the waves, plunging into the depths with a haunting grace. As the *Jolly Roger* sank and rose, its hull shimmered, transforming into a ghostly predator slicing through the seabed like a shark on the hunt. Coral reefs and sunken wrecks flashed past, their lifeless forms a stark contrast to the unnatural vitality of the spectral ship.

The crew cheered, their ghostly voices rising above the cacophony of the storm. The *Jolly Roger* surged forward, an unstoppable force driven by hunger and malice, ready to claim whatever lay ahead in the abyss. Unseen and unrelenting, it chased the faint glimmers of souls caught between life and death.

"Captain Hook, looks like we found ourselves the mother load." Smitty rubbed his hands together as if he was looking at a feast.

"Another large ship went down? Are we in the Caribbean again?"

"No sir, this ship is in the Atlantic. It is plum snapped in half. Men, Women, even children are stuck down here." Smitty's toothy grin glinted in the glow of a jelly fish.

"Seems like just our luck. Round them up!" Captain Hook's lips twisted up in a half toothy grin.

"Aye Captain."

Before the souls knew what was happening, five hundred and seventeen of them were now locked in the belly of the *Jolly Roger*. "Sir, we have five hundred and seventeen souls, seventeen of them children to young adult. None as clean and pure as we hoped for, but still they should fair us a good price, sir."

"Come now, why so few? That vessel had to have well over a thousand souls die on it." The captain looked hard at the name of the ship: *the Titanic*. "See here, I know that ship had almost two thousand people die in a crash. Some did not die on this ship but because of it." Hook's grin grew, knowing the truth behind the ship and the bounty on its lost souls.

The sunken ship now full of lost souls, calling out for help, rose from the depths until it was left floating on the surface. The sea covered in a dense fog, and the winds pushed the ship back to Skull Rock. It was not long before the crew moored the lines and set anchor.

The once sunny skies of Neverland grew cold and dark, causing the boys to wake and take notice.

Peter huddled with the Lost Boys in their hidden fort, his eyes sharp and unwavering as he gave his orders. "Stay here, where it's safe. The fort is protected; nothing can harm you within these walls." His voice was firm, but a shadow of doubt flickered in his expression. Tinkerbell hovered nearby; her light dimmed as if mirroring his unease.

"But, Peter—" one of the boys began, his voice trembling.

"No," Peter cut him off, his tone softening. "I'll be back before you know it. Trust me."

With that, he flew into the night, his silhouette a fleeting shadow against the pale moonlight. Tinkerbell trailed close behind, her tiny form casting faint sparks in the darkness. As they soared above the treetops, Peter's sharp eyes caught sight of a sinister procession below.

The pirates were marching, spectral figures herding a line of souls toward Skull Rock. The children's faces were pale and tear-streaked, their small hands clutching at nothing as they were driven forward. Peter froze mid-air, a cold dread gripping his chest.

"Tink," he whispered, his voice barely audible. "What are they doing?"

Tinkerbell's glow dimmed further. "There's nothing you can do," she murmured, her voice laced with sorrow. "They're the reapers of forgotten souls, Peter. Those children... they've been lost too long. The veil can't hold them anymore."

Peter's fists clenched as he watched helplessly. The line of children disappeared into the gaping mouth of Skull Rock; their terrified screams swallowed by the abyss. A curtain of black mist descended over the entrance, silencing everything, the sight chilling him to his core.

"We have to do something," Peter said, his voice trembling with frustration.

Tinkerbell shook her head, her light flickering weakly. "We can't. Not yet. This is their domain."

Peter hovered in silence; his heart heavy with helplessness. The screams of the children echoed in his mind, a haunting reminder of the fragile line he walked between defiance and duty. Above him, the storm raged on, a cruel reflection of the turmoil in his soul.

Anger and pain washed over Peter's face as he hatched a plan of action.

In a flurry of brilliant light, Tinkerbell flew into the air waving her wand, her little fairy mouth going so fast not even Peter could keep up with her.

"Come on Tink, let's have ourselves an adventure." And with that, Peter dove for the pirate ship. Taking his knife out, he cut the main sail from top to bottom, while Tinkerbell dusted the few children left with pixie dust, and their once dimly-lit souls shone brightly with hope once more.

Peter flew around them, calling, "Join hands and believe in me! I need you to believe and think of your families." He grabbed one boy by the hand, and they all linked together and were high in the sky before the pirates could return to collect them.

"Captain!" Smitty cried out, pointing to the figures flying over the moon.

Captain Hook looked into the sky and said, "So, dear boy, that's the game you want to play. Oh ho, then let the games begin."

LOST BOYS

Peter Pan flew the children to the heart of Neverland, guiding them into an open field where the soft glow of twilight stretched across the sky. The air was thick with a sense of wonder, but also a lingering sadness—these children were no longer just lost; they were waiting.

As they landed, the children hovered around Peter, eyes wide with curiosity and fear. Whispers passed among them, voices trembling with uncertainty.

"Who is he?" one of them asked, her eyes darting to Peter as she pulled her coat tighter around her small frame.

"And what is she?" another child whispered, pointing at the small glowing figure beside Peter.

Peter grinned, a mischievous twinkle in his eyes. "Peter Pan, that's what they call me," he said, his voice a mix of warmth and mischief. "And I promise you, if you just believe—truly believe—you'll never be lonely here again."

He gestured to the tiny, sparkling fairy beside him, her wings flitting like soft whispers of wind. "Tinkerbell is here to help me, and I'm here to help you."

The children stared, some skeptical, others wide-eyed with awe.

Peter's words seemed to hang in the air like a promise, one that perhaps they had longed for but never dared to believe in.

Tinkerbell flicked her wrist with a flourish, and in an instant, a staircase made of shimmering, icy crystal appeared before them, leading upwards into the fading light. The children gasped in awe, their voices rising in a chorus of questions.

"What is that?" one of the boys whispered, his voice trembling.

"It's stairs, silly!" another child giggled, but her voice faltered. "But where does it lead?"

Peter's expression softened as he knelt down to their level, his voice quiet and reassuring. "I need all of you to close your eyes and remember what it felt like to be happy... to believe in something greater than yourself." He smiled gently as the children hesitated. "Trust in that happiness. And trust me. The way will be shown when you're ready."

The children stood in silence, eyes wide, hearts pounding. Some were unsure, but they had nothing left to lose.

"Are we ready?" a little girl asked, her small voice uncertain, as she looked up at the stairs.

"I don't know..." another boy muttered. "I know they're reapers like me, but...I'm not like them."

Peter's eyes flickered with understanding. He had seen this before, the way children held on to their fears and doubts. He could feel their reluctance in the air.

A small girl, her face pale and her hair messy from the journey, took a tentative step toward the stairs. As her hand brushed the icy surface, the staircase seemed to come alive, bathing her in a soft, white light. She gasped as a soft voice echoed from above.

"I've been waiting a long time for you, Samantha."

The child's face broke into a radiant smile, her eyes filling with tears. "Momma!" she cried, her voice a mix of joy and relief. Without hesitation, she ran up the stairs, her small feet making quick, joyful strides. Each step she took seemed to make the light grow brighter, until, in an instant, she was gone—vanished into the light, as if the world had opened up just for her.

The others stood still, watching with a mixture of awe and confusion. One boy, his voice shaking, took a hesitant step forward. "Where did she go?" he asked. "Where did the light go?"

Peter's gaze softened, his voice taking on a sorrowful edge.

"Sometimes, when we're not ready—when we haven't truly believed—the stairs won't light the way. Not until we're ready ourselves." He placed a comforting hand on the boy's shoulder, feeling the weight of his words.

"What about me?" the boy asked, his voice barely a whisper. "Are you going to take me back to those men? Those... walking dead?" The fear in his voice was palpable, his hands trembling.

Peter crouched down in front of him, his expression kind but serious. "No, silly," he said with a smile that didn't quite reach his eyes. "You get to stay with me." He glanced at Tinkerbell, who nodded quietly. "What's your name?"

The boy looked away, his eyes clouded with confusion and pain. "I... I don't have one. They... they never gave me one."

Peter's eyes darkened for a moment, then softened again. He gently reached out and ran his fingers through the boy's sandy blond hair, a gesture so tender it made the boy's heart ache. "Curly," Peter said quietly, a name that felt right. "You can stay with me. You'll help me look after Neverland, and one of your jobs will be to help me guide the rest of these children to the other side. We'll make sure Hook and his crew never find us."

Curly's eyes were wide, but there was a flicker of hope there. "Curly?" he asked, a little laugh escaping his lips. "How original. But.. it works."

Peter smiled, his heart swelling with pride. He patted Curly on the back and watched as the boy walked to one of the other children, a small girl whose face was filled with the same fear that had once clouded his own. He took her hand, his fingers trembling as he led her toward the staircase.

49

The moment his hand brushed against the icy steps, the light returned—bright and warm. The child, her face now illuminated with a mix of awe and wonder, took a few hesitant steps forward. Two steps.. and then she was gone, swept away into the light.

"Someone must have been waiting for her," Curly whispered, his voice thick with emotion. He smiled softly, but there was a sadness in his eyes, a yearning for something more. "I guess... I guess it's my turn to help them."

Peter watched the children, his heart heavy with the weight of the responsibility ahead. He knew the road would be long, and there would be many more lost souls to help cross over. But for now, he was ready.

Curly turned back to him, a small but genuine smile on his face. "What now?" he asked, his voice full of hope.

Peter smiled, his eyes alight with mischief and determination. "Now, we take care of Neverland. Together. Wait until you meet the twins! We are going to have so many adventures."

Tinkerbell started to bristle her wings, jabbing Peter in the chest with her finger. Finally, she landed in his open palm. Peter held her close to his ear, sensing her unease.

"Peter, he is a lost boy. Lost boys are meant to be—"

"Free!" Peter interrupted; his voice sharp. "No one deserves the wicked fate that lies within Skull Rock."

He shuddered at the name, his voice softening as he spoke it aloud. "Even the name is evil. Let him be my lost boy, with Timmy and Tommy."

Tinkerbell's wings drooped; her voice low with concern. "Death will not be happy. All souls have a time to be claimed before they are subject to the bounty."

Peter's expression hardened as he looked to the horizon, where Skull Rock loomed ominously. "We'll deal with that when the time comes. But no child deserves to be lost forever, Tink. Not Curly. Not any of them."

"Peter, you did a bad thing for a good reason. Just be ready when Death comes to call on you." Tinkerbell's words drifted away as she flew off.

LESSONS

Peter flew off, tears stinging his eyes as they blurred the night sky around him. The wind whipped against his face, carrying the ache of his emotions. Ahead, a bright light appeared, glowing with an intensity that forced him to shield his eyes.

In an instant, the light engulfed him, and he found himself standing on a dark, sinister street filled with overturned trash bins and scurrying rats. The air reeked of neglect and decay.

In the shadows, Death loomed over an elderly woman slumped against a dumpster, while nearby, a younger couple argued in hushed, heated tones.

"She's been missing since Friday, and you're not worried?" the woman whispered harshly, her voice trembling with frustration.

The man's voice was icy, devoid of empathy. "She's old. It's about time she died."

The woman's face twisted with horror. "She is your grandmother!"

"Yeah, and when she dies, I'll inherit my father's company. We won't have to work another day in our lives. Finally, we'll live the life we deserve, Stacy."

Peter's heart clenched as he absorbed the scene. His feet carried him toward Death almost instinctively, confusion painted across his face. "Death?"

Death turned slightly, acknowledging him with a nod. "Peter, walk with me. I'm working, but we need to have a serious conversation."

"But—"

"Peter," Death interrupted, gently but firmly.

Reluctantly, Peter followed, his head bowed like a child about to be scolded. "Yes, Death."

Death's golden eyes locked onto Peter's as he extended a hand, lifting Peter's chin. For the first time, Peter saw something more than darkness in those eyes—a flicker of warmth, like sunlight breaking through a storm.

"Peter, your soul is still clean," Death began. "But you must be careful. Neverland is not just for you. It's a sanctuary for other reapers to rest."

"But—"

"I understand," Death interrupted again. "The cries of the children weigh heavily on you. You crossed most of them over, and I'm proud of you for it. But, Peter, when a reaper takes from another's charge, it can create conflict. Hook is not someone you want to antagonize. His ship of soul hunters is dangerous. Their souls are so dark, so corrupt, it will take an eternity for them to be redeemed. Unlike you Hook and his crew made a deal with—"

"The devil?" Peter's voice wavered. "I'm sorry, Death. I just couldn't stand their screams. Their cries for help were too much. Those lost boys," Peter bit into his bottom lip.

"Lost boys," Death mused, a faint smile playing on his lips. "I like that. Lost boys like you."

Death's gaze returned to the elderly woman. She was taking shallow, labored breaths, her frail form trembling against the cold. Peter hesitated, then stepped closer. Without a word, he rummaged through the nearby dumpster, pulling out a tattered blanket. He draped it gently over the woman and sat beside her.

Death's lips curved upward. "Always the gentle soul."

The old woman stirred, her eyes fluttering open. She reached out a trembling hand, placing it on Peter's. "Boy, why are you crying?"

"I'm not," Peter said, hastily wiping his tears.

"Ah, yes. Men must be tough, even in hard times," she said with a soft chuckle. Her gaze held a warm glow that made Peter's chest ache.

Peter glanced at Death. "Why can she see me but not you?"

"Some souls can sense a loved one from the other side," Death replied. "It's rare but meaningful."

"I've been waiting a long time for you." The old woman's grip on Peter's hand tightened. "Oh, sweet Peter, if you're here... does that mean Anna is here too?"

Peter's brow furrowed. "Who is Anna?"

"Anna is your mother," the woman said, her voice trembling. "She died bringing you, my first grandson, into this world. When I came to find you, your Uncle Henry told me you had died with her."

Peter's head snapped toward Death. "Is this true?"

Death nodded solemnly. "Peter, I brought you here to help cross over your grandmother. It's rare for me to bend the rules, but your courage and compassion for the lost boys earned you this chance."

Peter hesitated, his fingers tightening against the tattered blanket still in his hands. "You're my grandmother?" he repeated, the words tasting foreign yet strangely right.

Mrs. Adams smiled gently, her frail fingers brushing his cheek as if memorizing his face.

"I always hoped you'd grow into a kind boy, just like your mother. Anna was the gentlest soul I ever knew—always the first to laugh, the first to help. Losing her broke me, Peter. I spent years searching for you, thinking I'd failed her and Phillip both."

Her voice cracked as she spoke his grandfather's name.

She glanced at Death, a silent understanding passing between them, before looking back at Peter. "Phillip and I weren't perfect, you know. We had our struggles. But we loved Anna more than anything. And when she found out she was pregnant, she was so happy—"

Tears rolled down her wrinkled cheeks, the memories as vivid as fresh ink. "She told me she'd name her baby Peter, after the brother I lost in childhood. Did you know you were named for him? She said you'd carry on the joy he brought into our lives."

Peter's breath caught. "No one ever told me that."

"Your uncle..." Her voice hardened, and her hand gripped his tighter. "Henry always was a bitter man. When I found out what he'd done—telling me you were gone too—it nearly killed me. I wanted to fight him, but I didn't have the strength back then. I'm so sorry, Peter. I should've tried harder."

The street around them seemed to grow quieter, the shadows stretching longer as her words sank in. Even the arguing couple nearby had fallen silent, their harsh tones replaced by an uneasy stillness.

"Grandmother," Peter said softly, his throat tight with emotion. "It's not your fault. None of this is. You tried. That's more than most would've done."

Mrs. Adams gave a weak chuckle, her free hand wiping her tears. "You really are Anna's boy. Always so forgiving, even when you shouldn't be."

Death, standing just a step away, watched the scene unfold with an almost imperceptible softness in his gaze. When Mrs. Adams turned to him, her expression was firm, her voice steady despite the tremor in her hands.

"Mr. Death, I have one last request."

"Speak it," Death replied, his voice resonant yet patient.

"Promise me you'll look after my grandson. He's all I have left worth two licks of my family, and it eases my heart to know he's with someone who sees his worth."

Death inclined his head. "It will be my honor."

The golden door materialized then, its glow illuminating the grimy alley like a beacon of hope. Warmth spilled out, carrying the scent of lilacs and the faint hum of laughter. Mrs. Adams' face lit up as a figure stepped through the light.

"Phillip!" she gasped.

The man waiting for her was younger than Peter expected, his dark hair tousled as if by the wind, his smile wide and welcoming. He opened his arms, and Mrs. Adams surged forward with a strength that belied her frailty.

Peter watched as they embraced, their forms glowing brighter until they merged with the golden light. The door closed, leaving only the dim alley behind.

For a moment, Peter stood frozen, staring at the space where they had disappeared. The ache in his chest was both sharp and comforting—a bittersweet reminder of what he had gained and lost all at once.

"Death," he began, his voice breaking. "Why did you let me see her? Why now?"

Death placed a steady hand on his shoulder. "Because some lessons can only be learned by facing the past, Peter. She needed you, and you needed her. Take this moment and let it guide you. There will be more trials ahead. We may not know what awaits them on the other side of that door. It is not our place to rob them of their door."

Peter nodded, his jaw tightening. "I'll do my best."

Death's lips quirked into a faint smile. "You always do, Peter. Now, let's keep walking."

THE TRAIN TO NOWHERE

Snow fell lightly on the tracks, muffling the rhythmic clatter of the train as it wound through the barren plains. Peter stood at the edge of the spectral plane, watching the long, black locomotive snake its way across the icy expanse.

The whistle's mournful cry carried through the frozen night, a sound that tugged at Peter's chest. He knew what it meant: a child aboard that train was nearing the end of their journey—but not the one they expected.

Tinkerbell hovered at his side, her light dim and somber. "Why is it always the ones who hope the hardest?" she whispered, her voice like the chime of distant bells.

Peter didn't answer. Instead, he stepped forward, crossing the boundary between worlds. The cold of the mortal realm pricked at his skin as he landed softly in the last car of the train.

Inside, the air was stifling, a sharp contrast to the winter's chill outside. Rows of children sat on hard wooden benches, their faces pale and weary. Most were asleep, huddled under thin blankets, their small bodies swaying with the motion of the train. The air was thick with the smell of unwashed clothes and desperation.

Peter's gaze swept over them until it landed on a boy seated alone near the back of the car. He couldn't have been more than nine years old. The boy's face was gaunt, his cheeks hollowed from weeks of illness. Yet, he clutched a small toy horse in his hands, turning it over and over as though it were a talisman.

Peter moved closer, kneeling in front of the boy. "Charlie," he said softly.

The boy's head snapped up, his wide eyes locking onto Peter's. "Who are you? How do you know my name?"

"I'm someone who's here to help," Peter replied. "You've been so brave, Charlie. But your journey here is almost over."

Charlie shook his head vehemently, clutching the horse tighter. "No! I'm going to a new home. They said I'll have a family. I just have to get there." His voice cracked, and tears welled in his eyes.

Peter's heart ached. He reached out, but Charlie flinched away. "I know it's hard to understand," Peter said gently. "But sometimes, the promises they make don't come true. Sometimes, the journey we're on isn't the one we expect."

The boy's lips trembled. "I just wanted..I just wanted someone to love me."

Tinkerbell landed on Peter's shoulder, her soft glow illuminating Charlie's tear-streaked face. "You'll never be alone," Peter promised. "There's a place where you can belong. A place where you can be free to play and laugh forever. No more pain, no more sadness. Only adventure."

Charlie's grip on the toy horse loosened slightly. "Is it..is it far?"

"Not far at all," Peter said with a small smile. He held out his hand. "Come with me, and I'll take you there."

For a moment, Charlie hesitated. Then, slowly, he placed his tiny hand in Peter's. The world around them began to dissolve, the drab interior of the train car fading into vibrant landscapes. "Tinkerbell, you know the drill."

Peter extended his arm to watch as she walked to his fingertips and blew out a kiss of fairy dust that danced across Charlie's face.

"Okay Charlie, take my hand and we will fly to the second star on the right, then straight on to daylight and the dreamlike planes of Neverland. A place with lush green fields that stretch out beneath a sky painted with swirling colors, and a warm breeze that carries the sound of distant laughter."

In what was only a moment, a breath, they landed softly in Neverland. Charlie's eyes sprung wide as he took in the view of rolling hills and peaceful seas around them. When Charlie stepped forward, he was greeted by a matched set of eyes and smiles turned up in a mischievous grin.

"Tommy."

"Yes Timmy."

"Looks like Curly has a new friend to join us." Tommy smirked.

"Who is Curly?" Charlie asked, looking around.

"Me." Curly stood up, looking at the new lost boy to join the crew.

Peter watched; his smile tinged with sorrow. Tinkerbell flitted in front of his face, her light brighter now. "You did good, Peter," she said.

He nodded but said nothing, his gaze fixed on the horizon. The laughter of the Lost Boys echoed in the distance, but the weight in Peter's chest remained. For every child he guided to Neverland, the question always lingered: why did they have to leave so soon?

The moment was shortly lived as Peter and Tinkerbell felt another soul calling to them. Peter closed his eyes once more and they were off. The train whistle blew one last time, causing Tinkerbell to shiver in Peter's palm.

"Tink, we don't even get one child out of there and we're called back again. Do they not know how to look after these children or do they just not care?"

59

Peter walked into the compartment where they had just helped Charlie escape to witness the staff finding Charlie's cold lifeless body.

"Sir, we have another one." The gentlemen spoke softly to his superior. "You know the drill. Get rid of the body and all his personals," the older man stated as he walked on to the next compartment.

"Charlie, I am so sorry you never made it to the Midwest. I am sure the family would have loved to adopt you. Lord please take him into your arms, and please forgive me."

The man wrapped Charlie in his bedding, tying it off. He lifted Charlie up and carried him to the train car door. Under his breath, he uttered a silent prayer before he tossed Charlie's lifeless body out the door to tumble across the grounds under the night sky.

Peter turned away, ready for the next call. As he turned back toward the train, Tinkerbell tugged at his sleeve. "There's another one," she whispered, her light flickering urgently.

Peter scanned the car again and spotted a girl with tangled blonde hair seated near the middle. She cradled a tattered stuffed rabbit, its ears worn thin. Her eyes were fixed on the window, watching the snowy landscape blur past.

Peter approached cautiously, kneeling beside her. "Abigail," he said gently.

She turned to him, Startled. "Who are you? How do you know my name?"

"I'm Peter, and I've come to help," he said. "You've been so strong, Abigail, but this journey isn't taking you where you think."

Her brows furrowed. "They said I'm going to my aunt's house. She has a big farm with horses."

Peter hesitated, then reached out to touch the stuffed rabbit. "You love rabbits, don't you?"

She nodded. "I've always wanted to hold one."

"You will," Peter said, his voice soft with promise. "Where I'm taking you, you'll have all the rabbits you could ever dream of. You'll never be cold or hungry again. You'll be free."

Abigail clutched the rabbit tighter. "Is it real? Not just a story? Are you going to be a big brother for me?"

"It's real," Peter said, extending his hand. "Come and see. I can be your big brother. I never had a little sister before."

Her hand trembled as she reached for his. The train faded away, replaced by a field of golden grass dotted with fuzzy oversized rabbits.

Abigail's rabbit transformed into a real one, its fur flowing in the wind. She laughed with delight as she held on to him, the sorrow in her eyes replaced with joy. Then a staircase appeared before her, stopping her in her tracks.

"What is this?" she cried out.

"This is your door." Peter smiled as he took her hand, snapping his fingers so the rabbits would follow them to the stairs. The rabbits then climbed the stairs two steps at a time, causing Abigail to follow suit.

"Bunnies, wait for me!" Abigail giggled, then she suddenly stopped when she heard a voice that only she could recognize. "Momma!" she screamed, rushing up the stairs two at a time until she vanished into the white light.

PIRATE SOUL HUNT

The moon hung heavy in the night sky, casting an eerie silver glow over the endless expanse of the ocean, its pale light reflecting off the water in shimmering streaks like a trail of ghostly flames. The sea stretched endlessly before them, black and foreboding, as if the very depths were holding their breath.

The *Jolly Roger* sliced through the waves, its hull cutting through the water with a low, persistent hum. The sails billowed, filled by an unnatural wind that whispered through the rigging like the sighs of forgotten souls.

Captain Hook stood at the helm, his posture unwavering, his gloved hand gripping the wheel with a fierce certainty. His crimson coat flared behind him like a bloodstained flag of war. His eyes, dark and unblinking, scanned the horizon, ever watchful, as if he were searching for something—something just beyond the edge of the world.

The sea, it seemed, knew what he hunted. It churned beneath them, restless, its waves lapping hungrily at the sides of the ship as though eager to reveal its secrets. Tonight, it felt different, darker. The air itself felt charged with anticipation, as if the ocean was aware that Hook had come for what it hid.

The crew murmured among themselves, their voices low and tense, a constant hum of unease that rippled through the deck. It wasn't the first time they had sailed these cursed waters, seeking the souls of the lost—those spirits adrift in the void between worlds. But tonight, something was wrong. Each hunt had become harder, seemingly heavier than the last.

For some, it was the memories of past hunts that weighed on them. Faces of the lost; the ones they had dragged from the depths, mournful eyes forever etched in their minds, chasing them through their dreams, haunting their waking moments.

There were whispers in the night of crewmen who had not returned from the last hunt, their bodies never found, only their screams carried by the wind. Those who had gone in search of the lost souls on their own, now gone themselves, swallowed up by the very ocean they had once called their domain.

For others, it was the toll the hunt had taken on their captain. Hook's obsession had grown over the years, twisting and darkening, until even the men who once followed him with unwavering loyalty now found themselves questioning his sanity.

The pursuit of the lost had begun as a quest for power, a thirst for dominance over the spirits that roamed the seas. But now, it seemed, there was something deeper, darker driving him—the need for something that could never be found, a hunger that gnawed away at his very soul.

A strange unease had begun to settle over the crew. Each hunt felt like a step closer to something from which there could be no return. And as the years passed, it wasn't just the souls of the lost they feared—they feared the ship itself, and what it had become in the service of their captain's obsession.

The *Jolly Roger* had long since ceased to be just a ship; it had become a vessel for something far darker, carrying the weight of all those lost souls who had been claimed over the years.

As Hook stood at the helm, his sharp eyes fixed on the dark horizon, a quiet dread settled over him as well. It was a hunger that couldn't be satisfied, a thirst for power that had only grown over time. He knew the crew saw it, felt it too—the way he had changed, how the chase had come to consume him. And though he commanded their respect, there was a flicker of fear in their eyes when they looked at him now.

The hunt for the lost souls had once been a means to an end. Now, it was something far worse. It was a ritual, a compulsion. And Hook knew that with each soul they claimed, the cost grew ever higher.

No one spoke of it aloud, but the crew felt the weight of it; the price of their lives and their loyalty, the toll this endless chase had taken on their humanity. Each hunt weighed heavier because they knew the next might be their last. The sea, it seemed, never gave up its secrets without exacting a terrible cost.

Hook's gaze remained fixed ahead, the weight of the ocean pressing in on him. He could almost hear the whispers of the lost, feel their cold fingers beckoning from the depths. The crew stood in uneasy silence; the air thick with the unspoken fear that this hunt might be the one to claim them all.

"Bloody spirits, always crying out," muttered Smee, rubbing the back of his neck as if trying to rid himself of a chill. "Can't get their wails out of me head."

Another sailor, a gaunt man with hollow eyes, nodded grimly. "The kids we lost..they linger. Makes me wonder if we're cursed, Captain."

Hook's gaze snapped toward the crewman, his voice a razor-edged growl. "Cursed? By what? The sea?" He gestured broadly, his hook glinting in the moonlight. "No, you fool. We are her masters. She bends to my will."

"Begging your pardon, sir," the man stammered, "but their cries..it ain't natural. It's like they're calling us."

Hook's lips curled into a predatory smile. "Perhaps they are. And perhaps they should be grateful for it. You all know why you're here. We all have been damned to collect souls for him. He does not like it when souls escape his grasp. Were still hunting for one from long ago. It's been my mission shortly after I was damned."

The sea began to churn, its deep growl rumbling like a distant thunderclap, the waves rising and falling with unnatural speed, as if something monstrous stirred beneath them. The air thickened, heavy with salt and the bitter tang of impending chaos.

Hook raised his hand, his fingers rigid as if warning the very storm to halt, and the helmsman, eyes wide with dread, jerked the wheel sharply to starboard.

The *Jolly Roger* groaned—a low, mournful creak—as the ship fought against the swelling tide, its timbers straining under the violent push of the sea. The sails flapped violently, snapping like cracks of thunder as the wind shifted, howling through the rigging. Belowdecks, the old wood groaned in protest, a chorus of unsettling squeaks and groans as though the very ship feared what lurked below.

The hull shuddered, and with each wave that smashed against the ship's side, *the Jolly Roger* heaved and pitched violently, sending a cold spray of seawater sweeping across the deck. It stung against skin like shards of glass, the saltwater burning as it mixed with the bitter taste of fear that clung to the air. The waves—towering and relentless—seemed to press in from all sides, a constant crash that rattled the very bones of the ship, as though some unseen beast was prowling just beneath the surface.

Hook's eyes narrowed, his heart thudding like a drum in his chest as he stared into the maelstrom ahead. The water churned violently, the rhythmic roar growing louder, and for a moment, it felt as though the sea itself was alive—breathing, reaching—as if it wanted to pull them under.

"Captain, what are you doing?" Smee's voice wavered as the ship tilted precariously.

"The souls are restless," Hook said, his eyes gleaming with dark purpose. "Let's remind them who commands their fates."

The water beneath the ship began to swirl, its surface rippling and pulling inward with an eerie, almost deliberate slowness. The *Jolly Roger* groaned again, as though the very soul of the ship was trying to resist the unnatural force below.

The sea was alive, now—no longer merely wild, but conscious, intent on devouring. The whirlpool formed slowly at first, the center of the swirling vortex darkening, pulling the light from the surface, as if the very heart of the ocean was opening to swallow them whole.

The ship began to lurch violently to starboard, tilting with a force that sent men tumbling to their knees. The timbers creaked and groaned under the pressure, the sails shuddering as the wind howled in frantic, terrified gusts.

The ship's keel scraped against the water with a sickening, grinding noise, a sound that made the hairs on the back of the crew's necks stand on end, as though the very bones of the *Jolly Roger* were being scraped raw.

From beneath, a low, guttural roar began to rise from the depths— deep and muffled, like the growl of some great, submerged creature stirring from slumber. The whirlpool's pull became stronger, the water spiraling faster, and the sound of it was a deafening rush.

Like an endless, hungry wind, mixed with the dreadful splashing of water against wood, as though the ship itself were caught in a never-ending struggle to stay afloat.

Shadows danced within the depths of the swirling maelstrom—shapes twisting and writhing like tortured spirits, their forms shifting and blending; long, skeletal limbs reaching up from the darkened water, dragging at the edges of the whirlpool as though they longed to pull the ship into the abyss.

A chill swept over the deck, cold enough to bite through to the bones, sending shivers down the crew's spines. The air grew thick with the fetid scent of decay—of rot and death. A stench so overpowering it clawed at their throats and filled their lungs with the taste of the grave.

The crew recoiled, their faces pale, eyes wide with horror. The ship lurched again, harder this time, as though the very ocean was trying to tear them apart.

The wind shrieked as it tore through the rigging, and the waves crashed against the ship with such force that water poured over the sides, flooding the deck. It was no longer a storm—they were trapped in the grasp of something far older, far darker.

Hook's gaze fell upon the gaunt sailor who had spoken out earlier, gesturing with his hook. "You."

The man froze. "Captain, no. Please, I—"

"You questioned me," Hook said, his voice calm but laced with menace. "Now, let's see if you're brave enough to face what lies below."

Two other crew members grabbed the man by the arms, dragging him toward the edge of the ship. He thrashed and pleaded, his voice breaking with terror. "Captain, please! Forgive me. I have spoken out of turn."

Hook tilted his head, considering. "Yes, it appears you have. Now, if I allow this, will you do it again? Or do I need to teach this crew a lesson?" He stepped closer, his presence towering over the trembling sailor. "I can send you into the abyss. Let that Kraken of souls devour you."

The sailor's eyes widened as he peered over the edge. The whirlpool had become a vortex of pure darkness, tendrils of shadow reaching up as if hungry for life. Whispers of despair drifted upward, chilling the air.

Hook's voice dropped to a cold whisper. "Do you hear them? They're waiting for you."

The sailor fell to his knees, clutching Hook's coat. "Please, Captain. Have mercy."

Hook sneered, prying the man's fingers off with his hook. "Mercy is for the weak. And I have no use for weakness on my ship." He paused, his gaze hardening as he looked out over the crew. "Weakness invites chaos, and this ship thrives on order. You think the sea will show you pity? It devours the soft-hearted without a second thought. Remember that before you dare to plead again."

He nodded to the crew. "Throw him overboard."

The man screamed as he was dragged to the plank. The crew hesitated, their faces pale, but a sharp glare from Hook spurred them into action. They forced the man to walk to the edge, his pleas echoing across the sea.

"Captain!" one of the crewmen cried out, his voice quivering. "This isn't right. He's one of us."

Hook's eyes flashed with fury. "And he defied me. Do you wish to join him?"

The crewman shrank back, shaking his head. Hook stepped closer to the condemned man, his voice a venomous whisper. "Remember this moment. When the darkness takes you, know that it is your own cowardice that led you there."

With a final shove, the sailor plunged into the whirlpool. The crew gathered at the railing, watching as the man's screams were swallowed by the abyss. For a brief moment, the shadows seemed to writhe in satisfaction, and then the whirlpool stilled, the sea returning to an unnatural calm.

Hook turned back to his crew, his expression hard. "Let this be a lesson to you all. The sea is mine, and so are your lives. Do not forget it."

The crew nodded silently; their faces etched with fear. *The Jolly Roger* sailed on, its captain standing tall against the night, the weight of lost souls pressing heavily against the ship's timbers, as if their sorrow had seeped into the wood itself.

Each creak and groan of the vessel seemed to echo Hook's own inner torment—a relentless reminder that his ship was not merely a vessel, but a harbinger of despair, carrying both his burden and its grim purpose through the unyielding darkness.

VISITOR

Peter drifted through the swirling ether, a spectral figure moving from one lost soul to the next. Each child he encountered weighed heavily on his heart— a boy clutching a toy soldier as though it were armor against his fears, a girl cradling a threadbare doll whose sewn-on smile belied her sorrow.

Peter's words were soft, his touch lighter than a whisper as he guided them across the veil. For many, the path led to Neverland, though not always by his hand.

Lately, Peter had noticed an unsettling trend: other children appearing in Neverland without his knowledge. Confused, frightened, and utterly alone, they wandered its dangerous terrain.

Peter had caught fleeting glimpses of Death himself, shrouded in shadows, depositing these children without guidance. The sight gnawed at him. What were they meant to do there, left without help or protection in a place that was no longer the sanctuary it had once been?

Neverland had changed. The once-magical realm, a haven for the innocent, had become a battleground where the line between predator and protector blurred. Hook's influence had seeped into every corner, turning safe harbors into treacherous traps. Peter worked tirelessly to find these lost ones before Hook did, his efforts a desperate race against a growing darkness.

When he wasn't scouring Neverland, Peter found himself inexplicably drawn back to the hospital where his mortal life had ended. The once- overwhelming hum of suffering had been replaced by an eerie stillness, but its echoes lingered in the air like a haunting melody.

He drifted into the ward where he had once lain, his feet barely brushing the floor. The room was nearly silent, save for the faint, labored breathing of an elderly woman in her bed. Dr. Jacobson sat at her side, his hands steady as he adjusted her blankets, his face etched with quiet compassion. Peter's chest tightened. Even in death, he recognized the telltale signs of the Spanish flu ravaging her frail body.

In the corner of the room, Death stood cloaked in shadows, his skeletal presence both solemn and commanding. He turned a hollow gaze to Peter, his voice calm yet sharp. "Why are you here? You have no souls to claim."

Peter hesitated, his gaze dropping to the floor. "Sometimes...I need to ground myself. This place reminds me of who I was."

Death studied him for a moment, his form shimmering faintly. "Very well. Since you're here, so be it. But do not interfere."

Before Peter could reply, another figure appeared—a young woman cloaked in black with an air of brash indifference. She materialized like a storm, her boots clapping against the floor. Without hesitation, she pressed her hand to the old woman's chest.

The room darkened as a silver wisp rose—a fragile, shimmering light that twisted and flickered. The woman's eyes fluttered open, her voice weak yet clear.

"Wait...you're not my Peter," she whispered.

The reaper scoffed. "Peter who?"

"My sweet boy..."

The young reaper rolled her eyes. "Lady, you're old, you're dead, and you're on my list. Do you see a light? No? Okay, then. That means you're going to the Lost Souls Department. They'll give you a week to be claimed. If not—"

"She is not a lost soul!" Peter exclaimed, materializing fully.

The reaper turned sharply, her dark eyes narrowing. "Back off, kid. This soul is mine."

"Death!" Peter called; his voice steady but urgent.

Death shimmered into view, his presence filling the room. "Peter," he said, his tone warning. "I told you not to interfere."

"Boss, are you seriously letting this runt step in?" the reaper growled.

Peter ignored her, kneeling beside the woman. "Sister Agnus," he whispered. "It's me."

The old woman's eyes filled with tears as she reached for him. "Peter...Oh, my sweet boy."

He took her hand, his touch warm despite his spectral form. "Sister, listen to me. I need you to let go of any sorrow or pain. Think of your happiest memories—the ones that brought you joy."

The reaper scoffed. "This is ridiculous. Boss, he's bending the rules!" But Death said nothing, his gaze fixed on Peter.

Sister Agnus' trembling hand tightened around Peter's. "Seeing you...that's my happy thought."

Suddenly, a brilliant light filled the room. Golden stairs shimmered into existence, ascending into the Heavens. Sister Agnus' face lit up with wonder.

"You...you're an angel," she whispered, her voice trembling. "God sent you to me."

Peter shook his head, his own tears falling. "No, Sister. I'm just me."

She kissed his forehead, her frail body growing lighter as her soul glowed. "Thank you, my sweet boy."

With one last radiant smile, she ascended the stairs, her figure disappearing into the light.

The room fell silent. The reaper scowled, muttering under her breath as Death lingered; his gaze heavy on Peter.

Peter nodded, his chest tightening with a mix of sorrow and peace. He turned back to the empty bed, the faint echo of Sister Agnus' voice lingering in his mind.

The room fell silent, as Peter stood frozen, his chest heaving. The gruff reaper crossed her arms, glaring. "Well, that's just great. Now the higher-ups are gonna be all over me for losing a soul."

Death stepped forward; his skeletal face inscrutable. "Enough," he said, his voice like a whisper and a roar all at once. He turned to Peter. "You walk a fine line, child. Be careful not to cross it." Then he said to the reaper, "You are fine, she crossed over so you did not lose a soul."

Peter nodded; his heart heavy. "I couldn't let her go to the Lost Souls Department. She didn't deserve that."

Death's gaze lingered on him. "You remind me too much of myself when I was young. But be warned—compassion is a double-edged sword. It will either make you or break you."

"Death, why is Neverland changing?"

"Neverland is always changing, Peter. If you would have allowed my young reaper to do her job, Sister Agnus would have ended up in Neverland, however brief a time it would have been. I warned you not to interfere.

"Regarding the concerns in your heart about that constant battle with Hook over souls: you started that fight with him. So if you don't want him claiming the children, keep them away from Skull Rock. You will be fine, Peter. Keep up the good work. I am proud of you."

As Death and the other reaper vanished, Peter found himself alone once more. The hospital walls seemed darker now, the air colder. Yet, a faint warmth lingered in his heart—a flicker of light in the growing shadows. Peter nodded, his chest tightening with a mix of sorrow and peace. He turned back to the empty bed, the faint echo of Sister Agnus' voice lingering in his mind.

His hands clenched into fists as he whispered, "I'll protect them all. No one will end up lost."

THE SHADOW WITHIN

Neverland's skies darkened to a creeping gloom, unnatural even for twilight. The wind had fallen silent, the usual symphony of rustling leaves and distant laughter replaced by an eerie stillness. Peter felt it—a tension in the air, heavy and suffocating, like a storm ready to break.

He had been searching for a boy he'd seen crying near the mangroves when the chill began. It wasn't the crisp, playful cold of a Neverland evening but something deeper, something wrong. The sensation slithered along his skin, tightening like a noose around his chest.

Pausing mid-flight, Peter scanned the dense jungle below. The treetops swayed slightly, though no wind stirred them. Then he saw it—a shifting, inky shape slinking between the shadows.

At first, he thought it was nothing more than a trick of the light. But then it moved, too fluidly, too purposefully. Tendrils of darkness rippled out like grasping hands, and Peter's stomach twisted. The shadow left a dark stain in its wake, its path leading back to Skull Rock.

"Not good," Peter muttered, darting downward. He found the boy huddled beneath the gnarled roots of a massive tree, clutching a tattered blanket and a dirty teddy bear. The small frame shook with quiet sobs, each one breaking through the silence like a fragile whisper.

"Hey," Peter said softly, crouching beside him. "It's okay. I'm here now."

The boy looked up, tear-streaked face pale and frightened. He opened his mouth to speak, but a guttural growl cut through the air, low and resonant, vibrating the ground beneath them.

Peter's head snapped up. The shadow was closer now, emerging from the undergrowth. It writhed and coiled, a formless, menacing void.

Its presence filled the space with an unnatural cold, and Peter's breath misted in the air. Standing, Peter placed himself between the boy and the creature, fingers brushing the hilt of his spectral dagger. "Stay behind me," he ordered, his voice steady despite the racing of his heart.

The beast stopped, its tendrils spreading like roots across the ground, pulsing with dark energy. A hissing, rasping sound emerged—a mix of Hook's cruel tone and something older, deeper.

"Peter Pan," it hissed, disdain dripping from every syllable. "You have stolen what does not belong to you."

Peter's grip tightened on the dagger. "They're not yours to keep, Hook—or whatever you are. Neverland isn't your playground. It's a refuge."

A sound like nails scraping glass echoed through the air—a cacophony of rage and mockery. "A refuge for what? Lost souls? Broken dreams? This island is mine. These children are mine. *You* are mine."

Peter gritted his teeth. "I don't belong to anyone. Especially not you."

The creature surged forward, a wave of darkness crashing toward them. Peter dove aside, rolling to his feet with a sharp slash of his dagger. The blade glowed faintly as it struck the shadow, carving through it like mist.

The beast recoiled, screeching, but its form quickly reassembled.

Tendrils lashed out, striking toward Peter with terrifying speed. Twisting and spinning, Peter kept just ahead of the attacks, but the beast's presence grew heavier, its movements faster and more deliberate.

It's feeding, Peter realized. *The boy's fear, his loneliness—it's making the shadow stronger.*

"Think of something happy!" Peter shouted over the chaos. "Anything that makes you smile!"

The boy whimpered, clutching his blanket tighter. "I... I don't know how," he whispered.

The shadow beast hissed in delight, its tendrils closing in. Peter darted forward, slashing again, but this time the beast caught his arm. The tendril wrapped around him, icy and suffocating, and Peter felt his strength begin to drain.

"Do you feel it, Peter?" the beast rasped. "The despair. The emptiness. It's always been there, waiting for you. For all of you."

Peter struggled, his heart fluttering weakly as the cold seeped into his core. Memories flashed through his mind—his final days in the orphanage, the cold hospital bed, the fear of dying alone.

"No," Peter growled through clenched teeth, refusing to let the darkness win.

Closing his eyes, he forced himself to remember something brighter: Sister Agnus' smile. The golden stairs. The laughter of the Lost Boys. The warmth of guiding a child to peace. A faint glow began to emanate from his chest, spreading outward, growing brighter like the first rays of dawn.

The light grew stronger, brighter, pushing back against the shadow.

The beast shrieked, releasing Peter and recoiling from the light, its form beginning to falter.

Peter landed on his feet, his dagger glowing with golden energy. He stood tall, his voice steady. "You don't belong here," he said. He bent down, picking up the teddy bear from the ground. Dusting it off, he hugged it. "Here, now your teddy holds a little piece of my love and happiness. Give him a hug, and he'll share it with you." Peter smiled at the boy.

The shadow beast let out a final, piercing screech before retreating into the jungle. But as it vanished, Peter caught a glimpse of its core—a swirling, pulsing void filled with hatred and despair. Hook's voice echoed from within, cold and mocking.

"You can't protect them forever, Peter. The shadow will always be there, waiting. This beast has a hunger that can never be filled. Surrender, my boy, and maybe—just maybe—the shadow will show you mercy."

As the forest fell silent, Peter turned back to the boy, kneeling beside him. "It's gone," he said gently, his words warm like honey.

The boy hesitated, then nodded. A faint smile broke through his fear, and Peter felt a surge of relief. "Here, here now—the world is made of faith, trust, and pixie dust." Reaching into a small pouch on his hip, Peter sprinkled a pinch of dust over the boy, who began to float.

"Let's get you back to the others," Peter said, lifting the boy into his arms.

As they flew toward the hideout, unease lingered. The shadow beast wasn't just another threat—it was a warning. Neverland was changing, and the battle for its soul was only just beginning.

"Well, little guy, what's your name?" Peter asked as they soared above the jungle.

"Dylan, but Mommy calls me D."

"Well, D, do you think you can think of something that makes you happy?"

"Yes! Mommy and Daddy."

Peter smiled. "Good. Think of them for me." Slowly, he let go of Dylan, allowing him to fly on his own.

"I'm flying!" Dylan exclaimed with joy.

"See? All you need is faith, trust, and a pinch of pixie dust." Taking Dylan's hand, Peter led him the rest of the way to the hideout.

ECHOES OF DESPAIR

Peter perched on a distant branch; his usually radiant face shadowed with doubt. Below him, the Lost Boys bustled around the clubhouse, their laughter echoing faintly through the trees.

Normally, he would have joined them, leading their games with boundless energy. But today, he stayed back, his thoughts heavy and tangled like the vines creeping up the trunk of his perch.

He ran a hand through his auburn hair, sighing deeply. The laughter below felt wrong somehow—too sharp, too fragile. Once, it had been the sound of freedom. Now, it carried an edge of desperation he couldn't ignore.

A faint glow caught his attention as Tinkerbell fluttered toward him, her light dimmer than usual. She landed softly on his knee, her tiny face etched with worry.

"Peter," she began, her voice tinged with urgency. "We need to talk." He didn't meet her gaze, his eyes fixed on the group below.

"I know, Tink," he murmured. "The number of Lost Boys keeps growing."

"And that's the problem," Tinkerbell snapped, crossing her arms. "Peter, it's not just about numbers. It's about the island. It's cracking."

Peter frowned, finally looking at her. "Cracking? What are you talking about?"

Tinkerbell hesitated, her wings flickering uncertainly. "Peter, Neverland isn't infinite. Every soul that comes here pulls at its seams. You've been bringing more boys than the island can handle."

"I didn't bring all of them!" Peter shot back, his voice defensive. "They come here on their own. I just—" He faltered, guilt threading through his words.

Tinkerbell's glow dimmed further as she stepped closer. "Peter, why do you think that beast escaped Skull Rock? The balance of Neverland is breaking, and it's because of us."

Peter stiffened, his jaw tightening. "Hook sent it, didn't he?" Tinkerbell shook her head.

"No, Peter. That thing is older than Hook—older than you, older than me. It's part of the island, and it wants what you're refusing to see: balance."

Her words struck him like a blow. He leaned back against the trunk, his mind racing. Memories of the shadow beast's haunting words surfaced, chilling him to the core.

"I..I don't understand," he stammered. "What am I supposed to do? Tell the boys to leave? I can't abandon them, Tink. They're mine to protect!"

"And if you keep them here, you'll lose them all," Tinkerbell said sharply. Her wings flared, and she fluttered up to his eye level. "This isn't a game, Peter. Neverland isn't your playground any more than it is an escape from the truth. It's your responsibility to help them cross over. Lingering lost souls will only attract the shadow."

Her words hung in the air, sharp and unyielding. Peter clenched his fists, his heart pounding with frustration.

Far in the distance, a hollow laughter echoed through the trees, low and menacing. Peter's breath hitched as he looked toward the horizon.

"Time's running out, Peter," Tinkerbell whispered. "Decide what kind of leader you want to be, before it's too late."

Peter's eyes remained fixed on the horizon, his usual bravado nowhere to be found. The weight of her words pressed on him, heavier than anything he'd ever felt before. Below, the Lost Boys called for him, their voices filled with trust.

But for the first time, Peter wasn't sure he deserved it.

Peter's gaze lingered on the treetops as the hollow laughter faded into the distance. A cold wind rustled through the leaves, carrying whispers that seemed to come from the very soul of Neverland.

He shivered, but it wasn't the chill that unnerved him—it was the weight of something unseen pressing down on the island.

"Peter?" Tinkerbell's voice softened; the sharpness replaced with concern. "You've been different since you saw it, haven't you? The shadow beast?"

Peter's hands tightened around the branch. "It spoke to me, Tink," he admitted, his voice barely above a whisper.

Tinkerbell's wings stilled and her glow flickered. "What did it say?"

Peter hesitated, the memory clawing at his mind. "It said...'Your kingdom crumbles because you refuse to grow.'" His voice cracked, and he shook his head as if to banish the words. "What does that even mean?"

Tinkerbell hovered closer, her tiny hand brushing against his cheek. "Maybe it's time to stop running from the truth, Peter. Maybe it's time to grow up."

His eyes snapped to hers, anger flaring. "Grow up? That's what the shadow beast wants? To turn Neverland into the same miserable place the boys came here to escape from? No. I won't let that happen!"

Tinkerbell flinched at his outburst but didn't back down. "And what happens when Neverland collapses, Peter? What happens to them then? Growing up does not mean growing old Peter. You should already know that since you have passed on, you won't age. Growing up means accepting death as part of life. You need to help them grow up, Peter. They need to accept their fate."

She gestured toward the Lost Boys below, their laughter now faint whispers carried by the wind.

Before he could respond, a distant cry shattered the tense silence. Both Peter and Tinkerbell turned toward the sound, their eyes narrowing.

"That came from the northern forest," Peter said, his voice low and urgent. Without another word, he leapt from the branch, his body moving with the practiced ease of someone who had lived among the treetops his entire life. Tinkerbell zipped after him, her light cutting through the shadows.

The forest grew darker as they ventured deeper, the thick canopy blocking out what little light remained. The air grew colder, and Peter's heart raced. He hadn't felt this kind of unease since the shadow beast had first appeared.

"Peter, wait!" Tinkerbell called; her voice tinged with fear. "This part of the island—"

A rustling sound interrupted her, and Peter skidded to a halt. The underbrush ahead trembled, and a figure stumbled out, collapsing onto the ground.

It was one of the Lost Boys—a younger one named Charlie. His face was pale, his breathing ragged. He had long claw marks down his arm where a beast had attempted to hold him.

"Charlie!" Peter dropped to his knees, his hands gripping the boy's shoulders. "What happened? Who you hurt?"

Charlie's eyes fluttered open, but they were filled with terror. "I..I saw it," he gasped. "The shadow..it's coming for us. It said..it said we don't belong here. It..it said he is here to claim what is lost. The wheel of fate must not be stopped. A lost soul must be taken into the darkness where it will remain."

Peter's stomach twisted. He glanced at Tinkerbell, whose expression had turned grim.

"Peter," she said softly, "The island is trying to warn you."

"No," Peter said firmly, shaking his head. "It's not the island. It's that beast. It's trying to scare us, to break us. He is trying to take away my family!" He looked back at Charlie, his voice steadying. "You're safe now. I won't let anything hurt you."

Charlie nodded weakly, but his fear didn't fade.

As Peter helped him to his feet, a low, guttural growl echoed through the forest. The sound was impossibly close, and Peter froze.

"Peter..." Tinkerbell's voice trembled.

Emerging from the shadows was a creature like the one Peter had recently seen. It was massive, its form shifting and flickering like smoke caught in a storm. Its eyes burned with an unnatural light, and its maw twisted into a grotesque grin.

"Keeper of the Lost," the creature rumbled, its voice reverberating through the trees. "Your kingdom is built on lies."

Peter stepped in front of Charlie, his heart pounding but his gaze unwavering. "You don't belong here," he said, his voice defiant.

The creature's grin widened, revealing rows of jagged teeth. "Neither do they," it hissed, its gaze shifting to the trembling boy behind Peter. "This world lacks balance. A balance you yourself are at fault for not keeping. Hook may have given up taking back what you stole from me, but I am not as forgiving."

Tinkerbell darted in front of Peter, her glow intensifying despite her fear. "Leave him alone!" she shouted. "Peter is a good soul; that is why you can't touch him. Your darkness reeks and I can smell it from here."

The creature chuckled; a sound that made the air grow colder. "This is just the beginning, Peter Pan. Your games are over. Prepare to face the truth." With that, the creature dissolved into the shadows, its laughter lingering long after it had vanished.

Peter stood frozen; his fists clenched at his sides. Tinkerbell hovered silently beside him; her glow dim once more.

"Peter," she said softly, "we can't keep ignoring this. The island is changing, and if you don't act—"

"I know," Peter interrupted, his voice low and filled with a determination she hadn't heard before. He turned to Charlie, his expression softening. "Go back to the clubhouse. Stay with the others and don't leave until I say it's safe."

Charlie hesitated but nodded, disappearing into the trees.

Peter watched him go before turning back to Tinkerbell. "If the beast wants a fight, I'll give it one. But I won't abandon the Lost Boys. Neverland is their home, and I'll protect it no matter what."

Tinkerbell's eyes glimmered with both pride and worry. "Just promise me you won't try to do it alone."

Peter didn't answer. Instead, he looked toward the horizon, where the distant laughter of the shadow beast seemed to mock him. "Tink, it's time to fly, it's time to crow, it's time to fight."

ROSE WARD

The dim light of the hospital's oil lamps flickered against the cold stone walls, casting long shadows that danced across the corridors. The heavy scent of antiseptic mingled with the faint, sweet aroma of dried flowers that Sister Joy had arranged near the entrance—a small effort to bring comfort to a place burdened with despair.

Dr. Jacobson stood near the central table of the ward, adjusting his spectacles as he reviewed patient charts. The sound of soft, purposeful footsteps caught his attention, and he looked up to see Sister Joy approaching, her hands folded neatly before her.

"Sister Joy," Dr. Jacobson said warmly, his face breaking into a rare smile. "I'm so glad you decided to come on as one of my nurses."

She dipped her head modestly, her veil shifting slightly with the motion. "Dr. Jacobson, it is my honor to follow in Sister Agnus' footsteps," she said softly. "The convent was so saddened to hear of her passing. She was a light to us all."

Jacobson's smile faltered, a shadow crossing his face. "She was a remarkable woman," he said, his voice heavy with loss. "I know it wasn't an easy choice for the mother superior to allow her to leave the convent, but her calling to care for these children was undeniable."

He paused, his voice thickening. "It's why I fought so hard to bury her next to Peter. They belonged together, in spirit if not in life."

Sister Joy's eyes glistened as she looked up at him. "You knew about Peter?"

"Of course," Jacobson said, his tone softening. "He was the heartbeat of this ward. And Agnus...she saw him as more than just a patient."

A faint smile touched Joy's lips. "Doctor, who doesn't know about Peter?"

Their conversation was interrupted by the sound of hurried footsteps and muffled sobs. A well-dressed couple entered the ward, the woman's face streaked with tears as her husband clutched her arm, whispering futile words of comfort.

Dr. Jacobson stepped forward, his expression shifting to one of professional concern. "Are you all right?" he asked gently.

The woman shook her head violently, a wail escaping her lips. "No!" she cried, her voice breaking. "Doctor, please—we've just received the most terrible news."

Her husband spoke, his voice strained but measured. "Our three children...they've fallen ill. We came here hoping for help, but another doctor—Dr. Anderson—refused to see them without demanding an outrageous payment upfront."

Jacobson's expression darkened. "Where are your children now?" he asked, his tone laced with quiet urgency.

"On the Rose Ward," the man replied bitterly. "Where else would they be? We were told this hospital only has one ward for sick children."

"Not quite," Jacobson said, gesturing around. "The Rose Ward is reserved for wealthier families. This," he continued, his hand sweeping over the crowded room filled with cots and pale faces, "is the ward for those less fortunate—or those who have no one."

Mary, the woman, stepped forward, her tearful eyes scanning the room. "George," she said firmly, her voice soft but resolute, "we must."

Her husband nodded, understanding her unspoken plea. "Doctor," he said, "if you'll take our children, we'll gladly accept your care. Dr. Anderson demanded $3,000—per child—just to look at them. It's unconscionable."

Jacobson's eyes widened. "He was going to charge you $3,000 just for an examination?" He shook his head in disbelief. "What are their symptoms?"

"Fever, fatigue, headaches, and vomiting," Mary replied, clutching her husband's arm. "At first, we thought it was just a common illness, but they've gotten worse every day."

"Let's go see them," Jacobson said, his voice firm.

The couple led the way to the Rose Ward, their pace quickening with desperation. As they approached, the sight that met them made Mary gasp.

Outside the ward, three children were huddled on a bench, masks covering their small faces. The eldest, a girl of about ten, clutched a younger boy tightly as the youngest—a toddler—rested limply in her arms.

"Wendy!" Mary cried, rushing to her daughter.

"They...they told us we couldn't stay," Wendy said, her voice trembling. "They said we had to pay or leave."

Mary knelt, wrapping her arms around her children. "Oh, my sweet girl. I'm so sorry."

Dr. Jacobson's lips pressed into a thin line; his anger barely contained. "Come," he said, his voice gentle but firm. "Let's bring your children to my ward. They'll get the care they need."

The family began to move, but their path was suddenly blocked by a tall, stern figure. Dr. Anderson stood before them; his face contorted with disdain.

"Dr. Jacobson," he sneered, "I see you're attempting to poach patients again. Need I remind you that families like the Darlings belong under my care?"

Jacobson stepped forward; his jaw tight. "By charging them $3,000?" Dr. Jacobson asked, his tone biting. "If they can't pay, then—oh, I get it. You're trying to weasel your way out of having to practice actual medicine."

His lips curled into a wry smile, and his words carried a dangerous edge. "You've turned this hospital into a marketplace, Anderson. These children aren't commodities!"

Dr. Anderson's expression darkened, but he quickly masked his frustration with condescension. "Well, good doctor, we both know you can't afford the Western medicine I offer. Perhaps your new little Sister can pray to her God instead. Though I doubt it will help—after all, wasn't that Sister Agnus' approach? A lot of good it did her in the end."

The insult struck like a physical blow, but Jacobson held his ground. "If faith means fighting for those who can't fight for themselves, then yes—I'll pray. I'll pray for these children, and for you, Anderson, because God knows you've lost your humanity."

Anderson scoffed, stepping aside with a mocking bow. "Do as you wish, Jacobson. But don't come begging for supplies when your ward collapses under the weight of your misplaced charity."

Jacobson froze, the words hitting him with brutal force. His fists clenched at his sides as a vein pulsed angrily in his temple. "Watch your mouth, Anderson," he said, his voice low and trembling with rage. "Agnus had more courage and compassion in her smallest gesture than you've shown in your entire career."

"Oh, I'm sure she did," Anderson replied with a smirk. "Too bad it didn't save her—or her precious Peter."

Jacobson stepped forward, his presence towering, his voice filled with a quiet but undeniable power. "Her faith wasn't about saving herself, Anderson—it was about saving the souls of others, even those as lost as you. She fought for these children, and she did it without asking for a single cent. You might call that a failure, but I call it a legacy."

Anderson's smirk faltered for a brief moment before he scoffed and stepped aside. "Do as you wish, Jacobson. But don't come begging for supplies when your ward begins to collapse."

Dr. Jacobson led the Darling family and their children back to his ward, where the atmosphere, though burdened with illness, carried a sense of resilience. Sister Joy had already prepared fresh cots, ensuring a space was available for the new patients.

IN THE DOCTOR'S HANDS

"Someone once told me you could bring someone back to life simply by remembering them," Dr. Jacobson murmured to the quiet room. His voice broke slightly as he added, "Oh, Sister Agnus, I know you sent them to me. I'll do my best to care for them. I pray you and Peter are finally at peace—laughing together somewhere far from all this."

His shoulders slumped as he removed his gloves, staring at the empty chair Sister Agnus had so often occupied. Her presence lingered in the small space—from the faint scent of lavender to the outline of her rosary beads and the carefully arranged stack of medical journals she had insisted on organizing. He closed his eyes briefly, her voice echoing in his mind.

Dr. Jacobson approached the toddler with gentle precision, his stethoscope already warmed between his hands to avoid startling the child. "So, who do we have here?" he asked with a reassuring smile.

The eldest boy stepped forward, adjusting his spectacles with an air of practiced maturity that seemed beyond his years. "His name is Michael," he said softly. "He's going to be five this fall."

"Oh, you don't say? Such a lively age," Dr. Jacobson replied warmly. He glanced at the young boy. "And what is your name, young man?"

"I'm John," he answered, his voice steady.

"You're very brave, John. I promise we'll take good care of you and your brother and sister."

Michael clung tightly to his teddy bear, the fabric worn and threadbare from years of use. His wide, fearful eyes darted to his sister, who stood stoically, her small hands clenched into fists at her sides. Mary Darling gently placed her youngest, Michael, on the cot, smoothing his sweat-matted curls. Wendy held John's hand tightly as Sister Joy approached, her warm presence soothing the children's evident fear.

Sister Joy knelt beside him, her soft, reassuring tone filling the space. "Well, John, it's a pleasure to meet such a responsible big brother. Let me take a look at you while the good doctor tends to your baby brother." She playfully ruffled his hair before letting her palm rest gently on his forehead. Her expression shifted slightly as she murmured, "Oh my, you feel feverish. Come on, sit down and I'll check your vitals."

John climbed onto the edge of the examination bed, his legs swinging idly as he waited. His brave facade wavered only slightly when Sister Joy placed a comforting hand on his shoulder.

"I'll fetch water and cooling cloths," Joy said, offering Mary a reassuring smile before glancing at Dr. Jacobson for further instructions.

Mrs. Darling watched anxiously, her hands wringing a handkerchief until the fabric twisted taut. "Dr.?" she asked, her voice trembling as if each word required effort. "How is he?"

Meanwhile, Dr. Jacobson focused on Michael, noting the toddler's flushed cheeks and labored breaths. He examined the child's throat, feeling for swelling, before gently pressing the stethoscope to his tiny chest. The rhythmic sound of his heart was steady but faint, and his breaths were rapid and shallow.

Jacobson paused, removing his stethoscope and offering a calm but direct answer. "Mrs. Darling, we have a mysterious illness sweeping this town, and your children are showing signs of it. I swear I will get to the bottom of this illness. Michael's fever is quite high, Mrs. Darling, and his respiratory rate is elevated. These are concerning signs, but we caught it early, which is promising."

Sister Joy glanced over at Dr. Jacobson. "John is also feverish, though not as severe. His heartbeat is steady but fast. I think he's managing better than his brother for now." Sister Joy took a cook clothe to his forehead with tender care

Mrs. Darling let a silent tear run down her face. "But you can save my babies?"

Jacobson nodded. "We'll start with reducing their fever and rehydrating them," he said. "Sister Joy, see if we can spare another dose of the fever tincture. And please, send word to Father Titus. He can assist with the supplies Anderson keeps hoarding."

Sister Joy nodded, her hands already reaching for the supplies. "Right away, Doctor."

Dr. Jacobson turned back to the child, his expression softening as he gently touched Michael's cheek. "You're doing so well, little one. Just hang in there for me."

Dr. Jacobson moved with practiced efficiency, examining each child thoroughly. He noted their feverish foreheads and labored breaths, quickly setting up medications to reduce their temperatures. Jacobson placed a hand on Mrs. Darling's shoulder. "We'll keep an eye on all three of your children. Michael will need the most immediate attention, but I want to make sure Wendy and John are stabilized too. I'll examine Wendy next."

Mrs. Darling's eyes filled with tears, and she nodded, her voice trembling. "Thank you, Doctor. Truly."

Jacobson smiled faintly, meeting her gaze. "No thanks are needed. We'll do everything we can to help them." Standing up with one last look at the children now being cared for by Sister Joy, he said, "Mr. and Mrs. Darling, if I can have a quick word. Take your time. My office is on the corner."

Dr. Jacobson gave them a curt nod and strode to his office. He walked down the narrow hallway, where the hum of low voices and the faint beep of a distant monitor filled the air. The children's ward was quiet, save for the occasional rustle of blankets or the muffled cough of a restless child.

A soft knock interrupted his thoughts. Dr. Jacobson turned to find the Darling family standing hesitantly at the door. George's jaw was tight, his hand firmly gripping his wife's shoulder as if to steady her. Mary's eyes were rimmed red, her gaze flicking nervously between her husband and the doctor.

George's patience snapped, his voice cutting through the quiet like a blade. "Let me guess, good doctor, you've brought us back here to demand more money. Isn't that how these places work? Squeeze every last penny from families while offering false hope?"

"George!" Mary's tone was sharp, her eyes pleading with her husband to stop. Dr. Jacobson straightened, meeting George's glare with calm resolve.

"I understand your frustration, Mr. Darling. But I assure you, this isn't about money. It's about giving your children a fighting chance. They've been through so much already. Let's focus on what's important: their care and recovery."

George's jaw tightened, but he said nothing more. Mary reached for his hand, squeezing it as if to anchor him.

Dr. Jacobson met his glare calmly. "All your children are strangely sick."

George scoffed. "Thank you for telling us something we couldn't figure out for ourselves."

"GEORGE!" Mary screamed, her voice trembling with frustration.

George softened, pulling a pocket square to dab at his brow. "I'm sorry. I just can't stand to see my kids sick. We've already lost some family to polio this year. Then when we first arrived, we met that that money hungry leach." George paused, attempting to calm himself down.

"I understand," Dr. Jacobson said gently. "I'm not sure what this is yet, but I'll work day and night to figure it out. For now, I recommend that all three children stay here so we can monitor them closely. Michael is the sickest, and I've started him on IV fluids. I'd like to do the same for John and Wendy with your permission."

"Doctor, what are we talking when it comes to the cost of this care?" George had a faraway look as he attempted to calculate how to pay.

"Mr. Darling, I assure you that this isn't about money. Sister Agnus taught me that a long time ago." Dr. Jacobson pulled a handkerchief from his pocket and wiped away his stray tears.

Mary clutched George's arm, muffling a sob into her handkerchief. "Yes, Doctor. Whatever you need to do. I trust you, Dr. Jacobson. Let's go talk with the kids, George, and let the doctor get to work."

As they turned to leave, George stopped suddenly, coughing harshly. "Sir?" Dr. Jacobson stepped forward, his stethoscope already in hand. He listened to George's chest. "All your lung lobes are clear, and I don't hear anything of concern right now. Still, I suggest lots of fluids and rest. If your symptoms worsen, come back immediately. I'll keep reviewing my medical journals and analyze the children's symptoms. This illness is spreading, and I need to find answers." George nodded and led Mary out.

Sister Joy was gently tucking the children into their beds. IV poles stood beside each child, the fluids already flowing. Michael clung tightly to his teddy bear while sucking on his thumb.

"Children," George said, his voice steadying as he approached. "Your mother and I have spoken with the doctor. You'll need to stay here for a few days to get better." He looked at John. "Son, I need you to be the man of the family and watch over your sister and little brother."

"Yes, Father," John said, leaping from his bed. He grabbed his top hat and umbrella, pacing solemnly between his siblings.

"At ease, young Mr. Darling," Sister Joy said with a warm smile, setting a tray of food on the bedside table. "Children, eat up and then right to bed. Michael, how about you help me pick a storybook to read before bed?" Michael hesitated, glancing at his father and mother before nodding shyly.

Mary's eyes welled with tears. "Thank you, Doctor. I don't know how we'll ever repay you."

"Your children's health is repayment enough," he replied, offering a faint smile. Dr. Jacobson lingered by the doorway, watching Sister Joy's effortless care. She knelt by Michael's bedside, holding up a colorful picture book as he finally relaxed, his small body sinking into the soft mattress.

Soon, story time was completed, and Mr. and Mrs. Darling departed, but not before kissing the kids goodnight one last time. Sister Joy said, dimming the lamps, "You need your rest." She whispered a quiet prayer as she walked the Darlings toward the door. "Sweet night lights, protect these babes. Burn clear and bright; keep the Devil at bay tonight."

When at the ward's doors, she caught sight of Dr. Anderson locking up the Rose Ward. A shiver ran down her spine.

"Father," she murmured under her breath, "I dread the sound of his key in the lock. I am a good, God-fearing woman of faith, but I could swear that man is a marionette of the Devil." Sister Joy's gaze flicked to the Heavens briefly as she whispered a silent prayer.

When she finally stood, her eyes were tired but resolute. She returned to her desk, picking up a skein of midnight blue yarn and her crochet hook. With practiced precision, she began to work, the steady rhythm of the hook a quiet reminder that even in chaos, there could be peace.

Dr. Jacobson watched for a moment longer before turning away, his heart heavy but determined. He had made a promise, and he intended to keep it. He returned to his office to burn the midnight oil and save these children.

DR. ANDERSON'S SECRETS

The clinic office was eerily silent as Dr. Anderson locked the door behind him, the click of the latch echoing in the empty hallway. He adjusted his coat, fingers curling tightly around the keys in his hand. His expression twisted into something vile—a smirk that carried no warmth, only malice.

The lanterns flickered as he descended the narrow staircase at the side of the clinic. Each step creaked under his polished boots; the sound lost to the dense fog settling over the village outside. Turning sharply to the right, he ducked beneath the low archway that led to the cellar. The dim light illuminated the outline of a heavy wooden door embedded into the stone wall, its edges splintered and worn with age.

Dr. Anderson crouched, his gnarled fingers fumbling for a rusted skeleton key on the ring. With a grinding clunk, the lock gave way, and he pushed the door open. The hinges groaned as if mourning the entry, revealing a room steeped in darkness. A damp, cloying musk clung to the air, a sickly mixture of mildew, decay, and old blood.

Stepping inside, he struck a match, lighting a lantern hung on the wall. Its faint glow revealed a macabre tableau: jars of murky liquid filled with indistinguishable shapes, tools crusted with remnants of past use, and a bed in the far corner draped with a stained sheet.

Dr. Anderson moved toward the bed, his shadow long and distorted on the rough stone walls. He tugged on a pair of gloves, their latex snapping against his wrists, and tied a mask securely over his face. From the bedside table, he picked up a scalpel, its blade gleaming faintly in the dim light.

"Hello, William," he murmured, his voice low and gravelly. "Oh, how long it's been." He pulled the sheet back slowly, revealing the withered remains of a small boy. The Child's face was hollow, skin clinging like parchment to fragile bones. His limbs were ridged, contorted as if in silent protest of his fate. "I made your mother a promise, didn't I?"

Dr. Anderson's tone was almost conversational, his scalpel tracing a line down the corpse's brittle arm. "A proper funeral, she begged. But, you see, William, I couldn't bear to part with such a...valuable resource." He smirked, pressing the blade into the dehydrated flesh and slicing a sliver free. The sound was dry, like cutting through old leather.

He carried the sample to his makeshift lab at the other end of the room. The wooden table was cluttered with vials, powders, and glass beakers, each labeled in meticulous handwriting. He ground the fragment into a fine powder with a mortar and pestle, adding it to a jar with a practiced hand. "Just a little longer, my boy," he muttered. "Daddy needs to make a bit more money off these gullible fools."

Placing the jar back on the shelf, his eyes glinted with malevolent glee. "But you understand, don't you, William? I can't let you—or anyone—share my little secrets. So, no funeral for you. Not yet."

He turned back toward the corpse, his expression darkening. "Now, as for Sister Joy..." His voice dropped to a venomous whisper. "She's getting too close, just like dear Sister Agnus. Always asking questions, meddling where she shouldn't. I suppose it's time for her to fall ill." He chuckled, the sound hollow and chilling. "After all, if no one ever got sick, I'd be out of a job."

Dr. Anderson reached for a vial filled with a viscous, greenish liquid, holding it up to the light. "This should do nicely. A little drop here, a little sprinkle there. Before long, she'll be too preoccupied with her own survival to worry about mine."

He glanced back at the corpse on the bed. "Don't worry, William. You're safe with me—for now. But when the time comes, you'll help me again. You always do."

Blowing out the lantern, Dr. Anderson stepped back into the cellar's shadows, leaving the corpse behind as the heavy door creaked shut. The darkness swallowed the room once more, but the faint scent of decay lingered, a haunting reminder of the horrors concealed within.

Unseen in the shadows, a little boy hid, tears staining his cheeks. "Papa you promised Momma," he said, as the light surrounding him flickered and he blinked out of sight.

Sister Joy sat at her desk crocheting her blanket for little Michel while she gently hummed out hymns. The gentle rhythmic breaths could be heard across the ward. She looked at the clock; it was almost midnight. She stretched out, before saying one last prayer and resting her head on the desk.

A shimmer of light danced across the room, pulling Sister Joy from the edges of sleep. Her eyelids fluttered, and she sat upright, blinking into the dimly-lit ward. The light wasn't coming from any of the lanterns or the moon filtering through the high windows—it shimmered like morning dew kissed by the sun, yet it moved with intent, swirling and pulsing.

"Who's there?" she whispered, her voice trembling but firm as her gaze searched the room.

The light coalesced, its glow intensifying until it formed the outline of a boy, barely more than a wisp. His form was faint, his features translucent, but his eyes were unmistakably full of sorrow. Tears shimmered like stars on his ghostly cheeks.

"Miss Joy," the boy whispered, his voice carrying the weight of worlds. She gasped, clutching the rosary around her neck. "Who are you, child? What do you need?"

"I'm William," he said softly, his gaze falling to the floor. "Dr. Anderson hurt me..He promised Mama he'd take care of me, but he lied."

The blood drained from Sister Joy's face. She rose to her feet, her knees wobbling as her grip on the desk steadied her. "Hurt you? What do you mean?"

"He keeps me in the dark," William said, his small hand gesturing toward the floor. "And others too. He takes pieces of us, mixes them into his potions. He's..bad, Sister Joy."

The boy's form flickered, like a candle struggling against the wind. Sister Joy reached out instinctively, her hand passing through the light, a wave of cold tingling her fingertips.

"I'm scared," William said, his voice cracking. "He's going to hurt you too. He said so."

The weight of his words hit her like a blow. Sister Joy clasped her hands together, whispering a prayer under her breath. "Blessed Mother, guide me," she muttered, before returning her focus to the boy.

"What can I do, William?" she asked, her voice steadier now. "How can I help you?"

William looked up, his eyes brimming with hope and desperation. "You have to stop him, Sister. Before he hurts more people. Before he hurts you..please."

"I will," she promised, her resolve hardening. "I won't let him continue this..this evil."

The boy's form wavered again and he began to fade. "Thank you," he whispered as his light dimmed. "You're kind..like Mama said angels would be."

And then he was gone, leaving Sister Joy alone in the silence of the ward, the faint scent of lilies lingering in the air.

Her heart pounded as she gathered her shawl, her mind racing with what she had just seen and heard. She knew what she had to do—find proof of Dr. Anderson's crimes and protect the innocent lives in her care.

But as she turned toward the door, a low creak from the hallway made her freeze. Shadows moved just beyond the crack of the doorway, and the unmistakable sound of boots echoed in the stillness.

Dr. Anderson was coming, but for who, she did not know. Walking as quickly and quietly as she could, she went to secure the doors and windows to the ward. Once that was done, she knelt down to pray. Dr. Anderson's footsteps echoed down the empty halls, getting louder as he approached.

Sister Joy heard the doorknob twist but it failed to open. The jarring sound of the knob being twisted and shook abruptly stopped. His footsteps faded as he returned to the Rose Ward.

The lamps flickered again, casting uneasy shadows across the room. From those shadows, a child emerged, his form faint and spectral. Pain was etched deep into his features, even as a ghost, tears brimming in his eyes.

"Sister, please save them," William pleaded, his gaze sweeping over the ward and the rows of sick children. "It won't be long before their souls become his victims too. They're already sick—because of my father."

He hesitated, then pointed toward the Darlings. "Tell them I'm sorry. I never wanted any of this. Do you think God will forgive me?"

"Sweet William," Sister Joy said softly, her voice steady and filled with compassion. "God will not punish you for the sins of your father. I will pray you find peace."

Her words seemed to echo in the stillness of the ward, as a faint twinkle of light appeared outside the window. It grew brighter, until the window creaked open on its own. A young man stepped inside; his movements deliberate but cautious, accompanied by a flickering light that hovered near his shoulder.

The young man's gaze landed first on Sister Joy, then shifted to William.

"Sister Joy, are they here for me?" William's voice trembled, fear threading through every syllable. "No! I won't let them take me like my daddy did!"

With that, William vanished, his ghostly form blinking out of existence like a snuffed-out flame.

The young man landed softly on the floor, his footsteps barely making a sound. Sister Joy turned to him, her expression calm and unyielding. She took a bold step forward.

"Visiting hours are over, young man," she said firmly. "I don't know how you got in here, but you need to leave. Now." Without waiting for a reply, she spun on her heel and strode away, her words lingering in the heavy air.

ECHOES OF A SMILE

Thin curtains hung between the beds, offering the illusion of privacy but doing little to muffle the soft whimpers, coughing fits, and occasional cries that echoed through the ward. Pale moonlight streamed through the tall, arched windows, casting eerie patterns on the tiled floor. The room felt timeless, suspended between life and death, hope and despair, where every breath taken seemed like a fragile victory.

Peter stepped lightly, his soft leather shoes making no sound on the cold floor. His sharp eyes swept over the room, taking in the delicate forms of the children nestled in their beds. Some stirred restlessly, their faces glistening with fever, while others lay eerily still, their chests rising and falling in shallow breaths.

"Tink," Peter whispered, his voice barely audible but urgent. "Where is the boy we're looking for?"

Tinkerbell's flickering light hovering near him darted closer, her glow warm, yet frustrated. "Peter, I don't know. He was here—I *know* he was here!"

Peter sighed, his brow furrowing as he glanced at the endless rows of narrow beds. The faint metallic tang of illness clung to the air, mingling with the scent of disinfectant. It was the kind of place that seemed to devour happiness, leaving behind only shadows of what once was.

As he moved down the rows, his steps faltered when he stumbled upon the Darling children. Wendy lay peacefully, cradling her younger brother Michael in her arms, her expression serene despite the gloom of the ward.

Peter froze, his breath catching in his throat. For a moment, the noise of the ward seemed to fall away, leaving only the sound of Wendy's steady breathing.

"Tink, would you look at that," he murmured, his voice tinged with awe.

Tinkerbell fluttered closer, her light casting a soft glow over the siblings. "She's holding him like a doll," she said, her tone sharp with amusement.

"A living doll," Peter replied, tilting his head. "But why does she hold him so tightly?"

Before Tinkerbell could answer, a sudden cry shattered the quiet.

"Wendy! Wendy, the monster—it's going to eat me!" John thrashed in his sleep, his voice rising in terror.

Peter tensed, his hand instinctively reaching for the dagger at his side. His sharp eyes scanned the shadows, searching for the threat. "Tink," he hissed, "is the monster here too?"

The fairy sighed, her light dimming slightly as she landed on his shoulder. "No, Peter," she said gently. "He's dreaming."

Peter relaxed, though his gaze lingered on John for a moment longer. "Dreaming," he repeated softly, as if the concept eluded him. His attention drifted back to Wendy, and his expression softened. "There's something special about these children, Tink. I can feel it."

"Maybe," she replied cautiously, her wings fluttering faintly. "But we're here for the boy, Peter. Not them."

Peter nodded reluctantly, his gaze lingering on Wendy's sleeping form a moment longer before he turned away. As he stepped back into the shadows, he glanced over his shoulder one last time, his cheeks flushing faintly as he watched her rhythmic breathing.

Peter and Tinkerbell then slipped away, fading into the shadows like whispers in the dark.

Wendy's eyes fluttered open, her vision swimming in a purple haze that pulsed faintly, like ripples on water.

Blinking rapidly, she thought she saw a shadow dart across the room. The image lingered in her mind, even as her sight cleared. Shaking off the strange sensation, she glanced down and saw Michael had crawled into her bed at some point during the night.

A soft smile played on her lips as she scooped him up, cradling his small frame. She carried him carefully back to his bed, tucking him in as he murmured softly in his sleep.

Unable to return to sleep herself, Wendy wandered quietly through the ward. The faint hum of lanterns buzzed in the silence, and the cool tiles sent shivers up her legs with every step.

She stopped abruptly when she saw a boy standing alone by the tall arched window. His figure seemed almost ethereal, bathed in moonlight. His dark eyes glimmered with a knowing intensity that sent a shiver down her spine.

"You have his eyes," Wendy said softly before she could stop herself.

The boy turned toward her, his lips curving into a playful smile. "Who are you?"

Wendy straightened, smoothing the front of her nightgown. "Oh, pardon me. How rude of me." She dipped into a small curtsy, her voice trembling with the faint echo of childhood manners. "My name is Wendy Darling."

The boy tilted his head, his smile deepening as if he found her endlessly amusing. "And whose eyes do I have, Wendy Darling?"

She hesitated, glancing toward the desk at the far end of the ward. "The same eyes as the boy in the photograph Sister Joy keeps on her desk," she said finally.

The boy's smile widened, his face lighting up with a spark of mischief. "It's a pleasure to meet you, Wendy," he said. "But I can't stay. I need to fly, I need to crow, and I need to fight the night."

Before Wendy could respond, the boy dashed toward the window. With a single leap, he slipped through it and disappeared into the night.

"Wait!" Wendy called, rushing to the window. "What is your name?" She leaned out, her breath fogging the glass, but he was already gone. Her heart thudded in her chest as her gaze fell to the photograph on Sister Joy's desk. Slowly, she walked toward it, her fingers trembling as she picked it up. The boy's familiar smile stared back at her from the faded image.

Clutching the photograph to her chest, Wendy returned to the window. She let out a soft gasp when she saw something written in the condensation on the glass: P. P. & W. D.

Her lips parted, her heart skipping a beat as she traced the initials with her fingertips.

A voice whispered in her ear, "Peter Pan, that's what they call me."

The name echoed in her mind as she stared out into the night, a flicker of something new and unexplainable stirring deep within her. Her cheeks became flushed with embarrassment as she slowly walked back to her cot. She was met by Sister Joy, her expression soft but stern.

Wendy hesitated, holding the photograph tightly as Sister Joy approached. The older woman's expression was a blend of sternness and warmth, her voice a gentle reprimand.

"Young lady, it isn't proper to be out of bed at this hour. Come along now."

Wendy held out the photograph with trembling fingers, her cheeks warm. "I'm sorry, Sister Joy. I know I shouldn't have taken it, but...he looked so familiar. And he's..." She trailed off, her blush deepening.

"Cute, is he?" Sister Joy's tone softened, a wistful smile touching her lips. She took the photograph, glancing at it fondly. "Oh, yes. That's our Peter. He had a smile that could light up the whole ward, even in the darkest of times. He wasn't just a boy..he was magic." Her voice faltered, but she cleared her throat. "Now, enough of an old woman's memories. Into bed with you, Wendy. Let's keep you healthy and warm."

Peter Pan and Wendy Darling. A shiver coursed through Wendy, not from the cold, but from the feeling that her world was about to change forever.

WARNINGS IN THE DARK

Tinkerbell's light bobbed furiously as she hovered in front of Peter, her wings a blur. "What was the big idea writing on the window like that? Are you trying to get us caught?" Pixie dust scattered with each furious motion.

Peter leaned lazily against a tree, arms crossed, an unapologetic a smirk playing on his lips. "Caught? By who? A girl who talks to shadows and walks in moonlight?"

"Peter," Tink snapped, her glow flaring brighter, "she saw you. That's dangerous. Humans seeing you—interacting with you—complicates everything."

Peter waved her off with an easy grin. "Relax, Tink. She's just a girl. It's not a big deal," he said.

"Just a girl who's not dead," Tinkerbell shot back, folding her tiny arms. "Explain that one."

Peter's smirk faded, his expression growing thoughtful. "Yeah, I was wondering about that. How could she see me? Shouldn't I be... invisible to the living?"

Tink landed lightly on a nearby branch, her wings dimming. As she considered, her tone softened. "Children are different," she said, her voice quieter now. "They're not locked into what's real and what's not. Their minds are more open—freer. A child can believe in endless possibilities. That belief gives them a kind of... sight."

Peter's brow furrowed. "Okay, but what about Sister Joy? She's no child, and she told me to leave like I didn't belong there."

Tink hesitated. "I don't know. Maybe... maybe because she knew you in another life. Perhaps she knows you should have crossed over?" She shrugged, her glow flickering. "There's no time to figure that out right now, Peter. What matters is our charge. We were supposed to bring him here to set him free. Remember?"

Peter nodded, slowly, but his gaze lingered on the shadows of the forest.

"Something's off about that hospital," he muttered. "It felt darker than usual, like something was watching us. And that darkness..." He paused, his hand brushing the dagger at his side. "It felt familiar."

"Peter, don't go looking for trouble," Tink warned, her wings buzzing anxiously. "We don't have time for distractions. Hook is still out there, and if he finds the Lost Boys before we do—" She trailed off, shaking her head.

"I know." Peter's voice was quieter now, the weight of her words settling on him. He turned toward the small group of Lost Boys lingering nearby. Peter's feet touched the ground, his restless energy giving way to weariness. "Tink, let's sit and rest a while." He rubbed the back of his neck, his usual confidence dimmed by an unspoken weight.

Tinkerbell fluttered to a branch above him, her gaze scanning the forest. It was then that she noticed something carved deep into the trunk of a nearby tree. Her light dimmed, and a cold shiver ran through her.

"Peter," she called softly, her voice tinged with unease.

"What is it, Tink?"

Wordlessly, she pointed to the inscription, her glow illuminating the rough, jagged letters:

"If you are reading this, don't stop here."

Peter straightened, his eyes narrowing as he approached the tree. He ran his fingers over the deep grooves, his expression darkening.

"What does it mean?" he muttered, more to himself than to Tink.

"I don't know," Tink replied, her wings buzzing anxiously. "But I don't like it." She turned; her voice urgent.

Peter hesitated, but the panic in Tinkerbell's voice stirred him to action. He looked over his shoulder at the small group of Lost Boys who had accompanied them. "Tink, take them back to the treehouse. We need to go. Now."

"Peter…" Tink's voice was almost inaudible.

"Tink, take them back to the treehouse," Peter said firmly.

"What about you?" Tinkerbell's voice was filled with fear.

Peter's smile was thin but resolute. "I'll catch up. I need to figure out what's going on." His tone left no room for argument.

Tinkerbell hesitated, her glow dimming, but finally she nodded. She ushered the boys away, her wings fluttering faster than usual. "Be careful, Peter."

As Peter stood alone in the clearing, the forest seemed to shift and breathe around him, its shadows weaving together like a living thing. The gnarled branches of ancient trees reached out as if to ensnare him, and the air grew colder, heavy with an unnatural stillness. Darkness pressed against him, thick and suffocating, clawing at the edges of his resolve.

For the first time in what felt like an eternity, Peter felt the sharp prickle of fear creeping into his heart, unfamiliar and unwelcome. His gaze fell on a nearby tree, and his heart skipped. Carved into the bark were the jagged letters, their edges darkened as if burned. His fingers brushed the grooves, the warning sending a chill through him. "What does it mean?" he muttered aloud.

The forest answered with silence, but the weight of the inscription pressed down on him. Peter straightened, a flicker of unease darting across his face. He tightened his grip on the dagger at his side.

He clenched his fists, the memory of Tinkerbell's voice echoing in his ears. "Don't go looking for trouble." But trouble had a way of finding him, didn't it? He closed his eyes tightly, his breath hitching as he fought to steady himself. Think only happy thoughts.

But the thoughts that used to come so easily—mischief, laughter, daring exploits—slipped through his grasp like grains of sand. No longer was his mind filled with the thrill of games or the endless tricks he once played with the Lost Boys. That innocence felt distant now, like a star long faded from the sky.

Instead, his thoughts drifted, unbidden, to her.

Golden light kissed her skin, soft and warm, as if the sun itself had chosen her as its canvas. It was like dawn breaking over the horizon. Her voice—gentle and full of wonder—lingered in his ears, wrapping around him like a melody, rich and full, as if honey was poured over his soul. He didn't want to forget the way she looked at him, differently than anyone else ever had.

"Wendy," he whispered.

A faint smile tugged at the corners of Peter's lips, and his heart stirred with an unfamiliar ache, sweet and sharp all at once. Her name echoed in his mind like a whispered secret: Wendy.

Her name was the spark, causing warmth to spread through his chest, chasing away the cold. His feet left the ground, and he rose above the canopy. The shadows recoiled from the glow emanating from within him. For the first time in what felt like an eternity, he felt truly alive.

Peter opened his eyes and found himself floating in midair, the darkness retreating like a tide pulled back from the shore. The oppressive weight of the forest was gone, replaced by a quiet stillness. It was not the absence of sound, but a peaceful calm, as though the world itself was holding its breath. Peter felt something beyond the bounds of Neverland. Beyond his duties. Beyond even himself. He felt her.

With a triumphant crow, he soared into the sky, cutting through the clouds. Below him, Neverland stretched endlessly, its rivers and forests bathed in moonlight. The beach came into view, its sands untouched. No ship. No footprints. Nothing.

"Wendy Darling," Peter murmured, a wistful smile tugging at his lips. "You're my perfect storybook. Sorry Tink, keep the boys safe. For now, Neverland is safe. For now, I need to see Wendy."

Peter turned and flew back toward the hospital, his determination sharpening. He melted into the shadows just as dawn kissed the horizon.

DARKNESS

Peter landed silently in the dimly-lit ward, his form blending seamlessly with the shadows that stretched across the room. His sharp eyes took in every detail—the rhythmic hum of machines, the soft whispers of the staff, and the steady breathing of the children tucked into their beds. The air was heavy with the scent of antiseptic and worry.

From his perch in the corner, he spotted Sister Joy moving between the beds, her hands gentle as she adjusted pillows and smoothed blankets. Her face was serene but lined with concern. She stopped near Dr. Jacobson, who stood reviewing a chart, his brow furrowed deeply.

"Dr. Jacobson," Sister Joy said, her voice low but urgent, "did you see the reports in the paper this morning? The number of sick children is rising again. If we can't stop this..." Her voice cracked, but she swallowed hard and continued. "We'll lose them. All of them."

Dr. Jacobson sighed; his usually firm demeanor softened by exhaustion. "I know, Sister. We're doing everything we can, but it feels like we're fighting a losing battle. These children... they're slipping through our fingers."

As they moved from bed to bed, Peter followed their path with watchful eyes. Sister Joy leaned down to brush Michael's hair from his pale forehead, murmuring words of comfort, while Dr. Jacobson adjusted John's blanket, his expression weary. Peter's chest ached with an unfamiliar heaviness. He wanted to help—to do something—but he wasn't sure how. Not yet.

Suddenly, hurried footsteps echoed through the corridor. Peter tensed, his sharp senses pricking as Dr. Anderson entered the ward. The man's eyes darted nervously around the room, and his hand clutched a battered briefcase. He barely acknowledged Sister Joy and Dr. Jacobson as he moved quickly behind them, heading straight for Michael's bed.

From the shadows, Peter's keen ears caught the faint rustle of fabric as Dr. Anderson produced a syringe from his pocket. The man's hand trembled as he leaned over Michael and pressed the needle into the boy's arm. Peter's fists clenched, but he held his position, waiting; watching. Dr. Anderson moved to John next, repeating the act without hesitation.

When he reached Wendy's bed, Peter felt a surge of protectiveness.

Wendy had been the focus of his silent vigil, her steady breaths grounding him as he watched over the ward. Dr. Anderson raised the syringe, his movements jerky and frantic, but before the needle could pierce her skin, Peter reached out from the shadows and knocked over a metal cart. The trays clattered loudly to the floor.

The noise startled Dr. Anderson, who froze. Peter darted forward, his movements quick as a flash of light, and grabbed the syringe from the man's hand. "Not today, Doc," Peter growled, his voice low and sharp. Before Dr. Anderson could react, Peter sent him sprawling backward with a kick, the syringe shattering on the floor.

Wendy stirred, her eyes fluttering open. "Who's there?" she whispered groggily, her voice barely above a murmur.

Dr. Anderson scrambled to his feet, his face pale with terror, and bolted from the room. Peter didn't follow. His attention was locked on the two boys in their beds, their breathing shallow and labored. He turned and bolted from the room, nearly colliding with Sister Joy in the hallway.

"Dr. Anderson!" she exclaimed, stepping back in alarm. "What are you—" He grabbed her arm, his face inches from hers.

Pressing his body dangerously close to her, he hissed, "You saw nothing, Sister," his grip tightening, his eyes darting around wildly.

Sister Joy's eyes narrowed, a spark of steel flashing in her gaze. "And I feel nothing," she said coldly. "Get out of this ward. Now! Before I call the police."

Dr. Anderson released her as if her words burned him. Without another word, he turned and fled down the hallway, leaving her standing there, shaking.

In the ward, Wendy sat up, her face pale. She slipped out of her bed, her bare feet padding softly on the floor as she approached Sister Joy. "Sister," she said, her voice trembling, "that creepy doctor was just in my room. What was he doing?"

Sister Joy placed a calming hand on Wendy's Shoulder. "I know, child. I saw him creeping around, but I need you to return to your room now. It's going to be all right, I promise."

Before Wendy could protest, Dr. Jacobson ran up to them, his face a mask of urgency. "Sister Joy," he said breathlessly. "What is going on?"

"Dr. Anderson was here," she replied. "He ran out just now, acting strange."

Dr. Jacobson's frown deepened. "Something isn't right. I found him unconscious earlier, and now more children are slipping into comas without explanation. We need answers—fast."

Peter knelt beside Michael first, his heart hammering in his chest. The boy's skin was cool, and his pulse weak. A golden light began to glow faintly from Peter's hands as he reached into the small pouch tied to his waist. Inside was the finest pixie dust, shimmering and alive. He held a pinch between his fingers, letting it drift gently over Michael.

"C'mon, kid," Peter whispered. "Think happy thoughts. You can do this."

As the pixie dust settled on Michael, a soft warmth spread through the boy's body. His breathing steadied, and his cheeks gained a hint of color. Peter moved quickly to John, repeating the process. The golden dust sparkled as it fell, and the boy let out a soft sigh, his body relaxing into the bed.

Satisfied, Peter stood, his heart still racing. The boys were stable, for now, but the ward was far from safe. Peter coaxed the boys' spirits from their bodies, now free from the illness. "Come with me. We need to get your sister."

He returned to Wendy's room while the boys stood against the wall, waiting for her to return. Wendy walked in to find Peter sitting on her bed, and her wide eyes locked on him.

"Boy, what are you doing in my bed?" she asked, crossing her arms.

"Because it's your bed, silly girl," Peter replied with a grin.

"Don't make me call Sister Joy," Wendy warned, her tone sharp.

"Am I supposed to be scared?" Peter teased. Then his grin faded, and his voice softened. "There's something I need to tell you, Wendy."

"What?" she shot back, "that you're a creepy stalker?"

"Ouch," Peter said, feigning hurt.

"Who are you?" whispered Wendy, her voice trembling.

Peter hesitated, then stepped closer, the glow of the pixie dust reflecting in his mischievous grin. "Name's Peter. Peter Pan."

Wendy blinked, her brow furrowing. "Peter Pan? But... wait, *the* Peter Pan? The one Sister Joy said has died?"

"The one and the same," Peter replied.

Wendy stared at him, her face a mix of disbelief and confusion. "Oh, great. I must be hallucinating. First, I'm sick, and now I'm Imagining a cute boy in my room sitting on my bed."

"You're not hallucinating," Peter said firmly. "And you think I'm cute?"

Before she could respond, a soft gasp escaped her lips as Peter stood and sprinkled a faint shimmer of golden dust over her. "I'm here to help," Peter said with a wink. He held out his hand. "And I'm here to take you somewhere safe. You and your brothers."

"Safe?" Wendy echoed, glancing at Michael and John's bodies resting. "But... we can't leave. We're sick."

"Not anymore," Michael and John cried out, coming out of hiding.

Motioning to the golden glow still lingering around the boys, Peter said, "Pixie dust works wonders, but we need to leave before the bad guys come back."

Wendy hesitated, then slid out of bed, her bare feet touching the cold floor. She looked at her body on the bed, then to her brothers, who were standing before her while their bodies still rested peacefully. "All right. But only if they come too."

Peter's grin widened. "That was already my plan."

He reached into his pouch, sprinkling more pixie dust over Wendy and her brothers. "Now, think happy thoughts," he instructed. "Something that makes you feel light and free."

Wendy closed her eyes, a small smile forming on her lips as she thought of playing with her brothers in the garden before they fell ill. The golden dust began to swirl around her, lifting her gently off the ground. Michael and John followed, their faces lighting up with wonder as they floated beside her.

Peter grabbed Wendy's hand, leading her toward the window. "Ready to fly?"

"Fly?" Wendy gasped, her grip tightening on his. "Are you serious?"

"Always," Peter replied with a laugh. He pushed the window open, the cool night air rushing in. Beyond the hospital, the stars sparkled like a thousand promises waiting to be kept.

"Let's go," Peter said, his voice filled with excitement. "Second star to the right and straight on 'til morning!"

"Silly, it is morning," Michael giggled.

"So it is. So it is." Peter gently giggled. And with that, they soared into the early morning light, leaving the shadows of the ward far behind.

PINT-SIZED GREEN-EYED MONSTER

Peter held Wendy's hand tightly, his heart thundering in his chest as they soared through the twilight sky. Neverland unfolded before them, a kaleidoscope of colors and wild wonder. Michael gasped as a herd of wild horses galloped beneath them, their manes shimmering like liquid gold under the fading sunlight.

"Look, Wendy! Ponies!" Michael squealed, squirming excitedly in John's arms.

"Hold still, Michael!" John scolded, gripping his little brother more tightly as he tried to wriggle free.

Peter laughed as they approached the treehouse, its wooden structure twisting organically around a massive tree trunk. The Lost Boys, a mismatched assembly of grinning faces, burst from their hiding spots, cheering as Peter landed with the Darling children.

"PETER!" they shouted in unison, their voices echoing through the clearing.

Peter crowed, throwing his head back. "Cock-a-doodle-do!"

Wendy glanced around in wide-eyed wonder. "Peter, who are all these boys?"

"They're my Lost Boys!" Peter announced proudly, puffing out his chest. "The best gang in all of Neverland."

Michael wriggled free from John's arms and bolted toward the nearest pony, his high-pitched giggle trailing behind him. Wendy started to follow, but Peter's grip on her hand tightened.

"Peter," she said, her cheeks flushing slightly, "I really should—"

"Oh! Sorry!" Peter stammered, quickly letting her go, his face tinged with embarrassment.

Before Wendy could respond, a golden blur zipped into the clearing, buzzing with palpable fury. Tinkerbell's tiny wings beat so rapidly they seemed to hum, and she landed on Peter's shoulder with a stomp.

"Peter Pan!" she snapped, her voice sharp enough to silence the boys' chatter. "Where did you run off to without me? You know the rules—I go with you anytime you claim a child! And who are *these* people?" She gestured dramatically toward the Darling children, her tiny hands on her hips.

"This is Wendy, John, and Michael Darling," Peter explained, unfazed by her anger. "They're going to stay here with us!"

"Stay here?!" Tinkerbell's voice rose an octave, her face turning crimson. "Peter, you can't just bring anyone to Neverland! This is our place! They'll ruin everything!"

"Calm down, Tink," Peter said dismissively, turning his attention back to Wendy. "They're not going to ruin anything."

Tinkerbell's wings fluttered violently as she flew up, glaring at Peter. "Oh, sure. You always say that until they do! It was not that long ago we had to fight with the shadow beast. All because we were becoming overrun with Lost Boys."

Peter beamed as the Lost Boys swarmed around him, each clamoring for his attention. Wendy stood at the edge of the commotion, observing the boys with a mixture of amusement and curiosity. Michael toddled back from the pony, clutching a fistful of wildflowers, and John hovered protectively by his side, eyes wary.

Tinkerbell zipped into the air, her wings a golden blur as she fluttered toward Wendy. She landed lightly on a nearby branch, her arms crossed, glaring at the taller girl.

"What's she doing here?" Tinkerbell hissed, loud enough for everyone to hear. "Girls don't belong in Neverland!"

Wendy turned to face the tiny fairy, taken aback but keeping her composure. "I beg your pardon?" she asked, her tone polite but firm.

Tinkerbell smirked and flew closer. "You heard me. Girls have cooties. Right, boys?"

The Lost Boys broke into giggles and nods, but Peter frowned. "Tink, stop it," he said sharply. "Wendy's our guest."

Tinkerbell pouted but said nothing, the wheels in her mischievous mind already turning.

"Tink, is it?" Wendy's voice was smooth as glass as she stared down the pint-sized fairy.

"It's Tinkerbell to you," Tinkerbell hissed, narrowing her eyes that had a faint hint of greenish glow.

"Is the rule only real girls have cooties? From what I can see you are a girl but seem to be free of cooties. So if you're not a real girl, why would a real boy like Peter be interested in you?" With that, she turned to walk away but not before Tinkerbell flew at her with her miniature dagger held out.

"STOP!" Peter bellowed, stopping Tinkerbell in midflight.

Tinkerbell's eyes flared with anger as she zipped off to her hidden room in one of the knots of the willow's trunk. Like a spider in her web, she was plotting her next move to catch her prey.

The next morning, Wendy awoke to giggling and the faint sound of whispers. The Lost Boys, under Tinkerbell's instruction, had crept into the treehouse while she slept. Armed with paints made from crushed berries and mud, they planned to decorate her face with silly designs.

Tinkerbell hovered over Wendy's sleeping form, grinning wickedly. "Hurry up, before she wakes up!"

One of the boys reached forward with a smear of green paint, but Peter burst into the room just in time. "Hey! What's going on in here?"

The boys jumped back, scattering like startled mice. Peter crossed his arms, glaring at them. "What were you doing?"

"Nothing!" they chorused, though the paint-covered hands of one boy betrayed them.

Peter's eyes narrowed as he glanced at Tinkerbell. "Tink, enough. You can't keep picking on Wendy."

Tinkerbell stomped her foot in the air. "I'm just having a bit of fun!"

"Not at Wendy's expense," Peter said firmly. He turned to Wendy, who was now sitting up, looking bewildered. "Don't worry, I won't let them bother you."

Wendy smiled softly. "Thank you, Peter."

By midday, Tinkerbell was fuming. "If Peter's going to stop every prank, I'll just have to make this one foolproof!"

Later that day, Wendy wandered to the edge of the clearing, admiring the vibrant flowers and exotic plants growing wildly around the treehouse. As she leaned down to pick a delicate blue bloom, a faint giggle caught her attention.

The Lost Boys were crouched in the bushes nearby, whispering excitedly. Above Wendy, a precariously balanced bucket of water teetered on a branch, ready to tip.

Tinkerbell darted toward the boys, her voice a hushed squeal. "Now! Pull the rope!"

But just as the boy holding the rope gave it a tug, Peter swooped in, catching the bucket mid-fall and dumping the water harmlessly onto the ground. "Nice try, Tink," he said, his tone laced with amusement.

Wendy turned around, startled but unharmed. "Peter, what's going on?"

"Nothing!" Peter said quickly, shooting a warning look at the boys. "Just a little game."

Tinkerbell fumed, her tiny fists trembling. "You're no fun, Peter Pan!"

"Tink, Neverland is filled with fun. I am sure we can all find a way to play nice together."

Peter's words were sweet but firm, causing Tinkerbell to once again storm off to pout. In the open field, Peter watched Tinkerbell's retreating glow with a furrowed brow. Something about her anger lingered, an unease he couldn't quite shake.

Wendy, oblivious to the tension, smiled warmly at the Lost Boys, as Michael toddled back with a fistful of wildflowers, his giggles ringing through the air.

The sun was setting over Neverland, casting the landscape in shades of gold and lavender. Wild horses galloped along the horizon, their manes shimmering in the fading light.

The Lost Boys' treehouse towered above the forest; its twisting branches adorned with lanterns that swayed in the gentle breeze. The scene was perfect—idyllic, even—but Tinkerbell's mood was anything but.

Perched on a high branch, the fairy glared down at Wendy as she arranged the boys around the fire pit. They listened intently as Wendy's melodic voice wove stories about life in London. Even Peter, sitting cross-legged with Michael on his knee, seemed enraptured.

"And then Nana chased us all the way to the park," Wendy said with a laugh, her hands gesturing animatedly. "You should have seen her, bounding through the flowerbeds with my father running after her!"

The boys burst into laughter, clutching their sides. Even Peter's grin stretched wide, a sight that made Tinkerbell's wings tremble with annoyance.

"Why does she get all the attention?" Tink muttered to herself, her tiny fists clenched. "She's not that special."

In a flurry of glittering dust, Tinkerbell zipped down toward the group. She hovered just above Wendy's head, a mischievous smirk curling her lips. With a flick of her wrist, she sent a fine mist of pixie dust raining down onto Wendy's hair.

Unaware, Wendy continued her story. But soon, John's eyes widened, and he pointed at her. "Wendy! Your hair…it's glowing!"

Wendy's hands shot up to her head, her fingers tangling in the now shimmering strands. "Oh! What on earth?"

The boys erupted into laughter again, but this time at Wendy's expense. Peter chuckled, though he shot a glance at Tinkerbell, who tried to feign innocence.

"Tink," Peter said, his tone carrying a warning. "What did you do?"

"Me? Nothing!" Tinkerbell said, twirling in the air as if she had no idea what he was talking about.

Peter sighed and leaned closer to Wendy. "Don't worry, it'll wear off. Tink just likes to...express herself."

Wendy smiled politely, though a flash of irritation crossed her face. "Well, I suppose I should be flattered."

As Wendy helped Michael toast marshmallows, Tinkerbell zipped by and nudged the stick in Michael's hands, sending the marshmallow plopping into the fire.

Michael pouted, and Wendy quickly reassured him, grabbing another marshmallow to replace it.

Peter watched the scene unfold, his brow furrowing. He knew Tink's antics weren't harmless fun; they were deliberate. Standing, he intercepted her mid-flight, catching her between his hands like a firefly.

"Tink," he said, peering at her through his fingers. "What's gotten into you?"

Tinkerbell crossed her arms and turned her back to him. "Nothing! Maybe I just don't like her."

Peter sighed. "She's our guest. You can at least try to be nice."

"Why should I? She's stealing you from us!" Tinkerbell's voice cracked, and for a moment, Peter thought he saw tears glistening in her eyes. But before he could respond, she wriggled free of his grasp and flew off into the shadows.

Wendy approached cautiously. "Is everything all right?"

Peter forced a grin. "Yeah. Tink just needs time to...adjust. She'll come around."

Tinkerbell slipped from the shadows and whispered to one of the boys, handing him a small jar of sticky sap. "Put this on her seat. She'll never be able to get up!"

The boy hesitated but followed her orders, smearing the sap on Wendy's log while she was distracted. Tinkerbell mischievously snickered and flew to a nearby branch, eagerly waiting for the prank to unfold.

As Wendy approached the chair with a plate of fruit in her hands, Peter's eyes widened in realization. "Wait, Wendy—don't sit there! That seat's, uh... dirty! Here, sit over here instead." He gestured to another log, his smile innocent but knowing.

She paused, startled by his sudden outburst. Peter grabbed the chair and flipped it over, revealing the sticky mess.

Wendy gasped, while Tinkerbell let out an exasperated screech from a nearby branch.

Wendy blinked, slightly confused but obliging. "Thank you, Peter."

"Tinkerbell!" Peter scolded, his voice sharper this time. "That's enough!"

Tinkerbell crossed her arms, her glow dimming as she pouted. "I was just trying to protect you. She doesn't belong here, Peter. She's not like us."

Peter softened; his voice gentler but firm. "Wendy's my guest, Tink. And she's staying. You don't have to like it, but you do have to stop."

Tinkerbell let out an exasperated growl. "Ugh! Why do you always ruin my fun?"

After the third failed prank, Wendy decided she'd had enough. She stood tall, her hands on her hips, and addressed Tinkerbell directly. "Tinkerbell, I'm not here to replace you. I can see how important you are to Peter. I just want to be friends. Why do you hate me so much?" she demanded. "I've done nothing to you."

Tinkerbell zipped up to her, her eyes blazing. "You don't belong here! Peter's mine, and you're just a silly girl with no wings or magic!"

Wendy's cheeks flushed, but she kept her voice steady. "Peter isn't yours, Tinkerbell. He's everyone's friend. And for your information, I don't need magic to be important."

The Lost Boys watched in stunned silence as the two girls faced off. Peter stepped between them, holding up his hands. "Enough! Both of you!" He turned to Tinkerbell. "Tink, Wendy is my guest. You don't have to like her, but you do have to respect her."

Tinkerbell crossed her arms and huffed. "Fine. But don't come crying to me when she ruins everything."

Tinkerbell hesitated, her glow flickering uncertainly. For a moment, she looked as though she might say something, but instead, she turned and flew off in a huff.

Wendy sighed, shaking her head. "She's quite the handful, isn't she?"

Peter grinned sheepishly. "You'll get used to her." Then, running his hand through his hair, he added, "She'll come around eventually."

Wendy nodded, though her expression was uncertain. "I hope so."

The night ended quietly, with the Lost Boys drifting to sleep one by one around the dying fire. Peter sat at the base of the treehouse, staring out into the dark forest. Somewhere out there, Tinkerbell's light blinked faintly, a tiny star against the inky sky.

He sighed; his heart heavy with the weight of divided loyalties. "Why can't things just stay simple?" The shadows of Neverland seemed a little darker that evening, and he couldn't shake the feeling that something—or someone—was closing in.

In the distance, Hook stood at the bow of his ship, his gaze fixed on the treehouse. His hand tightened around the hilt of his sword as the sight of Peter filled him with loathing.

"Captain," came Smee's nervous voice from behind him, "are we going to—"

"Silence!" Hook barked, raising his hook to cut him off. His eyes gleamed with malice. "Soon. But not yet."

Suddenly, a flicker of light darted toward him. Tinkerbell, her rage uncontainable, perched herself on the brim of Hook's hat, her tiny form practically trembling with indignation.

"It's not safe for people to see us together," she whispered urgently into his ear, her voice low and conspiratorial. Her green eyes glinted with something dangerous.

Hook smirked, tilting his head slightly. "And yet here you are, my little firefly."

Tinkerbell's fists clenched as she stomped her tiny feet on the brim of his hat. "She doesn't understand him like I do!" she screamed, her voice shrill with jealousy. "She never will!"

Hook raised a brow, amused by her outburst. "Jealousy is unbecoming, my dear."

"I'm not jealous! And I am not your dear!" she snapped, though her tone betrayed her. "I'm just—protective."

"You are the spitting image of my sweet beloved—perhaps in another life," Hook mused.

Tinkerbell looked around wary of Hooks crew lumbering around mindlessly.

PIXIE

Tinkerbell hid within the plume on Hook's hat, her voice barely audible. "It's not safe for people to see us together."

Hook let out a soft chuckle. "Oh, I see. Are you and your sweet Peter Pan having a little spat? Now, as much as I'd love to stick it to that cheeky little bastard, you are his sprite. Death gave you to him, and I've no intention of stirring up more trouble with Death. Death and my master have their own battles let's not add to it shall we. I stick to my seas and the lost souls that find their way to me. That was my bargain, my penance."

"He's bringing people to Neverland that don't belong!" Tinkerbell's wings fluttered in rapid frustration, a faint shimmer of pixie dust escaping with every beat.

"Oh-ho-ho," Hook teased, leaning back with a grin. "That's his job, little one. To bring the lost souls here until they're ready to cross over. But now..if those souls were to wander out of his territory—maybe then—I might be tempted to intervene and collect a little one's soul here or there. But, as far as I can tell, he's done a fair job of keeping them in his domain."

"He brought a *girl*!" Tinkerbell's voice rang out, shrill and accusing.

"Well, last I checked, girls die too, you know." Hook plucked her gently from his hat and set her down on a whiskey barrel.

Tinkerbell paced furiously across the barrel's surface, her tiny feet tapping against the wood. "I don't remember seeing the Darling family on his list!"

Hook's brow arched as he dragged the edge of his hook along the metal band of the barrel, a shower of sparks flickering to life. "Oh? And if they weren't on his list, how exactly did he manage to collect them? Don't tell me he hasn't learned his lesson after that last incident with Death. I wonder which reaper he's pissed off this time."

"I don't think he stole from another reaper," Tinkerbell admitted softly, avoiding Hook's piercing gaze.

"Pray tell, little fairy, what's eating you, then?" Hook pressed; his voice edged with impatience. "I've no time for riddles, and it seems to me you're just jealous."

"Hook, I told you I'm just protective. Peter is my reaper. Wait, Hook, if I'm Peters fairy as a reaper." Tinkerbell paused and started to franticly look around.

"Oh, not all of us reapers are given a fairy, but I will say having one would make my job of claiming lost souls go faster. This lot of cod fish are slow at reaping. Do you think you want to change teams?" Hook gave a toothy grin as he twisted his mustache.

Tinkerbell froze mid-step, her glow dimming for a moment as Hook's words sank in. "Change teams? You think it's just that simple? You think I could just... abandon him?"

Hook smirked, leaning forward so his face loomed over her. "Why not? It's not like he owns you, sprite. Death might've given you to him, but Death also must love a good bargain. And I've got a few favors saved up maybe the big fellow, if you're interested."

"I'm *not* interested!" Tinkerbell snapped, her wings flaring out behind her like tiny blades. "Peter needs me. He's—" She stopped herself, clenching her fists.

"He's what? A reckless fool?" Hook offered, his voice dripping with mock sympathy. "Face it, fairy. The boy's been playing with fire ever since he took that deal. You think bringing the Darling girl here is bad? Oh, I'd wager it's worse than that. Much worse. Peter does not know what game he is playing it may already be too late."

"What do you mean?" Tinkerbell demanded, her tiny voice trembling now.

Hook leaned back, pulling a long, deliberate drag from his pipe. The smoke coiled around him like ghosts, making his face seem even more sinister in the dim light.

"Well, if she wasn't on his list, she doesn't belong. And if she doesn't belong, that means one of two things: either she's not dead...or she was stolen from someone else's."

Tinkerbell gasped, her hands flying to her mouth. "No! Peter wouldn't—he couldn't—"

"Couldn't? Oh, darling, we both know he *could*." Hook's voice was soft but cutting. "The question is, did he? And if he did, well...I'd say Death might not be too pleased about that, hmm? Nor would whomever he stole from."

Tinkerbell's wings drooped, the weight of Hook's words crushing her spirit. She wanted to defend Peter, to shout that he'd never do such a thing. But deep down, she couldn't be sure. Lately, Peter had been... different.

Distant. Brooding. She'd chalked it up to the burden of his responsibilities, but now she wasn't so sure.

"Why are you telling me this?" she asked quietly, narrowing her eyes at Hook.

"Because, my dear," Hook said with a wicked grin, "I like to keep things...interesting. And if Peter's little operation starts to crumble, well, let's just say I wouldn't mind picking up the pieces. Especially if those pieces include you."

Tinkerbell bristled, her glow flaring brightly. "You're disgusting."

Hook laughed, a deep, rumbling sound that echoed through the ship's hull. "Perhaps. But I'm also right. You're loyal to a fault, little one, and that loyalty might just be your undoing. Take my advice: find out what Peter's really up to. Before it's too late. I would hate for you to share his fate."

With that, he tipped his hat and turned away, leaving Tinkerbell standing alone on the whiskey barrel, her mind racing with doubts and fears.

As Hook's footsteps faded, she whispered to herself, "Peter...what have you done?"

Tinkerbell shot off and quietly returned to her knot in the treehouse. "Tink? Tink are you in there?" Peter's voice came out in hushed tones.

"What do you want, Peter? I'm sure you'd rather have Wendy." Tinkerbell's words burned like acid. She came to the opening with her arms crossed, eyes burning red from her tears.

"Aww, Tink, no one can replace you. Besides we have a job to do. I have more children we need to cross over." Peter pulled out a small book from his pocket. Written in golden letters were the names of four children.

"Peter! Why are we getting called for so many children?" Tinkerbell shook off the negativity that once hung on her like a cloak.

"Let's go and find out. Tink…" Peter grinned broadly, "let's have ourselves another adventure."

SERUM

Sister Joy went about her day fretting over the growing workload of children, rich and poor, both seeming to get sick and quickly slip into comas. With each passing child, she said a little prayer over them. "Dr. Jacobson, have you gotten any new leads on what is causing this illness?"

"Sadly no, Sister Joy." Dr. Jacobson's face was haggard from many nights of restless sleep. "I have spent so many hours working on finding a cure to an illness I know nothing about."

Mr. and Mrs. Darling walked into the unit, the stress of dealing with the sick children evident on their faces. They found Dr. Jacobson working on Michael, drawing samples and changing his IV port. "Doctor, how are my babies?" Mrs. Darling's voice was almost a whisper.

Mr. Darling stepped up with a steely look in his gaze. "You promised me Doctor."

"I know, but as you can see, it's not just your children. I can't seem to find the contaminant."

"Please hurry, Doctor. I don't know how much more of this my wife can take."

While the Darlings were visiting with Doctor Jacobson, Sister Joy excused herself to find some more supplies. Out in the hall, she heard Dr. Anderson, and she quietly ducked behind a tapestry hanging over the alcove that lead to the supplies. A dark gruff voice bellowed out, "Where you really spying on me?"

Sister Joy remained silent; her breath caught as she waited for him to leave.

"How dare you accuse me of spying on you?" growled a dark voice in reply. "If it was not for me covering up your mess with the last death, you would be facing a massive lawsuit."

"Let them try to sue. I have nothing to hide. I have them sign agreements so that I cannot be held liable if their loved ones do not make it."

Sister Joy clutched the folds of her habit, her fingers trembling as she pressed herself further into the shadows of the alcove. The dark voice continued, its tone sharp and unyielding, "I'm not sure how much longer I can keep this under wraps, Anderson. The deaths are piling up, and the board is starting to ask questions."

"And whose fault is that?" Dr. Anderson snapped; his voice tight with suppressed anger.

"You were the one who insisted we keep using the serum—said it was our best chance to stave off the illness. Now look where we are," the stranger's voice growled out.

"Aww, poor baby. Is your daddy getting to you?" Dr. Anderson's words stung like venom.

"You Promised me results; that's why we allow you to do your experiments. We pay you handsomely and we need results." A fist slammed into a palm, causing a loud slapping sound.

Sister Joy's heart pounded against her ribcage. *Serum?* Her mind raced, piecing together fragments of overheard conversations and fleeting glances at charts she wasn't supposed to see. She had suspected something wasn't right, but this.. this was confirmation.

"The serum wasn't ready," the dark voice hissed. "You knew that as well as I did. We were testing on assumptions." Dr. Anderson's smug smile could be felt with just his words.

"Assumptions! That is rich. And now the Darlings' children are at death's door, and their father is breathing down my neck." The younger man's patience was wearing thin.

"Then maybe we should tell the truth," Anderson said, his voice gravely. "Tell them we were under pressure from the investors. Tell them we tried—"

"You tell them nothing!" The dark voice cut him off, venomous and commanding. "If word gets out about what we've been doing—if they even *suspect*—we'll lose everything. Understand? Everything."

Sister Joy felt her throat tighten. She didn't understand all the pieces, but it was clear that the sickness plaguing the children wasn't entirely natural. She forced herself to breathe quietly, not daring to move, praying the tapestry would continue to shield her.

The voices grew quieter, and she heard the shuffle of footsteps. "What about the boy?" Dr. Anderson asked in a low tone. "Michael Darling. He's the worst off."

There was a pause. Then the dark voice replied, "If he doesn't make it...we ensure none of them speak. Ever."

Sister Joy's stomach churned. *Ensure none of them speak?* Her hands tightened into fists, rage and horror swirling inside her. Whoever this man was, he had no compassion; no care for the lives of these innocent children.

The footsteps retreated, and silence fell once more. Joy waited a few moments, her breathing shallow, before slipping out from behind the tapestry. Her knees felt weak, but her resolve was stronger than ever. She had to do something—anything—to protect these children.

As she gathered the supplies, and her thoughts, before she returned to the ward, her mind raced with the memory of the conversation. The sight of Michael's pale face only steeled her resolve further.

Mrs. Darling sat by Michael's bedside, holding his limp hand, her tears silently falling onto the bed linens. Mr. Darling stood at the foot of the bed, his hands clenched into fists as he stared at Dr. Jacobson, who was making notes on a clipboard.

"How is he?" Sister Joy asked softly, her voice betraying none of the turmoil within her.

Dr. Jacobson glanced at her; his haggard eyes filled with sorrow. "The fever isn't breaking. If we can't find the cause soon...we'll lose him."

Mrs. Darling let out a quiet sob, and Sister Joy placed a reassuring hand on her shoulder. "He's strong," Joy said gently. "And we're doing everything we can."

She couldn't bring herself to tell them the truth—not yet. Not until she had more proof. But deep down, she knew that time was running out.

That night, long after the lights in the ward had dimmed and the hushed stillness of the hospital settled in, Sister Joy knelt in the small chapel on the east wing. The flickering candlelight cast long shadows across the room, and the faint scent of incense lingered in the air. She clasped her hands tightly, her whispers echoing softly in the empty space.

"Please," she murmured, her voice breaking. "Guide me. Show me how to help them."

The candle closest to her flared suddenly, the flame stretching higher than it should have. Joy's eyes snapped open, her breath catching in her throat. The flame danced erratically for a moment before settling, and she felt a chill sweep through the room. She wasn't alone.

A figure emerged from the shadows near the altar a boy, no older than ten, with sandy hair and piercing eyes that seemed to glow faintly in the dim light. This was not William; this one was different. His presence was both unsettling and strangely calming; the boy oddly familiar. When he spoke, his voice was soft but carried an otherworldly weight.

"They're lying to you," he said, his gaze locking with hers. "The sickness isn't natural."

Sister Joy's heart pounded in her chest. "Who…who are you?"

The boy tilted his head, a small, enigmatic smile playing on his lips. "I'm here to help," he said simply. "But you have to trust me. Look where you dare not look. You will find what you seek but no one wishes to see."

Before Joy could respond, the boy turned and began to walk away, his figure dissolving into the shadows. The room grew still once more, and the candlelight returned to normal. Sister Joy sat frozen, her mind reeling.

Whatever was happening, it was bigger than she had imagined. And now, it seemed, she wasn't the only one trying to save the children. Now, she needed to find William, and she paused, trying to remember what he told her.

HEART STONE

The serene glow of Neverland's moon bathed the treehouse in silver light, casting long shadows through the wooden beams. But the peace was deceptive. In the farthest corner of the hollowed-out trunk, Tinkerbell hovered in her hidden nook, her wings trembling with frustration. Tiny hands clenched around the hilt of her dagger, seething as Wendy's laughter rang through the treehouse, her voice effortlessly commanding the attention of the Lost Boys—and worse, Peter.

"This isn't right," she whispered to herself, her luminescence dimming. "This isn't our Neverland anymore. He isn't my Peter Pan anymore. NO!" she screamed, stomping her feet. "Wendy, I was made for Peter. Can you say the same?"

But was he still hers? Peter had always been hers. She had kept him safe, kept him close. Yet here he was, looking at Wendy with something soft, something dangerous.

A shadow of doubt flickered through her mind. Maybe she had made a mistake. Maybe she should let Peter decide for himself. But then she caught the way he looked at Wendy—puppy-eyed, entranced. The same way he once looked at her. A sharp pang of jealousy struck her, and her tiny fingers clenched tighter around her dagger. No, she wouldn't lose him. Not to her.

There was a place, a forbidden place, where Peter never ventured—the Vale of Shadows. Legends spoke of spirits lurking there, lost children who had failed to heed the island's rules, their whispers filling the air like distant cries. A cruel smile curled on Tinkerbell's lips.

"If Wendy wants adventure, let's see how she handles real danger."

The next morning, the sun hung high, golden beams piercing through the dense canopy, as Tinkerbell flitted toward the river where Wendy, Peter, and the Lost Boys lounged in the midday warmth.

She forced a pleasant smile, letting her wings sparkle like scattered diamonds in the light.

"Wendy, dear," she purred, her voice dripping with false sweetness. "Since you love stories so much, I thought you might like to see something truly special. Ever heard of the Heart Stone?"

Peter's head snapped up, his relaxed posture stiffening. "The Heart Stone? Tinkerbell, that's in the Forbidden Forest. You know it's dangerous there."

Tinkerbell twirled midair, feigning innocence. "Oh, Peter. Where is your sense of adventure? You always said Neverland is about discovery. And Wendy has been so curious. It's only fair she gets to see the wonders of our world."

The Lost Boys perked up, eager. "Can we go too?" one of them piped up Peter hesitated.

He was about to say yes, when Tinkerbell darted forward, whispering into his ear, "Let's just be the three of us. We don't need distractions."

That was all it took, as Peter nodded slowly. "Fine. Just us."

Wendy's brow furrowed, glancing at Peter. "If it's truly dangerous, perhaps—"

"Not if you're careful," Tinkerbell interrupted, wings shimmering as she drew closer. "I'll guide you myself. Besides, Peter will come too. That is, if he's not afraid."

Peter's jaw tightened. Tinkerbell knew just how to prod him. He turned to Wendy, searching her face, but her curiosity had already taken root.

"I'd like to see it," she said, excitement lighting her features. "Imagine the story I could tell!"

By late afternoon, they set out. The deeper they ventured, the darker and colder the forest became.

The vibrant greens of Neverland dulled into muted shades, the air thickening with an unnatural stillness. Gnarled branches twisted like skeletal fingers, and the usual hum of life—birds chirping, leaves rustling—had fallen eerily silent.

The further they walked, the more Wendy felt a presence— something unseen, watching.

Peter, walking ahead of Wendy, cast a wary glance at Tinkerbell. "Tink, are you sure about this?"

"Oh, don't be such a worrywart," she replied, though there was an edge to her voice.

They reached the clearing of the Vale of Shadows, and there it stood— the Heart Stone. The jagged blue crystal pulsed with a ghostly pale light, shadows coiling around its base like smoke. The whispers started then, soft at first, curling through the air in a language none of them understood.

Wendy took a step forward, entranced. "It's beautiful." Then the visions came.

Faint, flickering images—her parents' worried faces in the hospital ward, her own body lying motionless. Then a shift—herself, older, cradling a baby in a dimly-lit room. The weight of the child in her arms felt real, the warmth of it pressing into her chest. Her breath caught. The image of two worlds, but one could not exist if the other existed.

Peter grabbed her wrist. "Don't touch it."

The whispering grew louder, as though responding to him, the tendrils of darkness slithering toward Wendy's outstretched fingers. Before she could react, the shadows surged, wrapping around her like liquid night. Wendy gasped, eyes widening in terror as an icy chill seeped through her skin.

"Wendy!" Peter lunged, slashing at the tendrils with his dagger. The shadows recoiled with an eerie wail, but they clung stubbornly, pulling Wendy toward the Heart Stone.

"Peter, do something!" Tinkerbell shrieked; all traces of smugness erased.

Peter didn't hesitate. He wrapped his arms around Wendy and pulled with all his strength, his heart hammering as the darkness resisted. "Wendy!" Peter cried out, causing her to turn her head to face him.

He leaned in and kissed her. With a final wretched cry, the shadows shattered apart, retreating into the stone. Wendy collapsed against Peter, her breathing ragged, her body trembling.

Silence fell over the clearing.

"W-what was that?" Wendy asked as she tried to regain her composure.

"That was a shadow," Peter started but was cut off when Wendy placed her hand over his mouth.

"You kissed me?" Wendy looked doe-eyed into Peter's eyes, as his face ran crimson.

"I...I guess I did. I never kissed a girl before." Peter broke eye contact and looked at the ground.

Wendy placed a hand on her own lips as her cheeks became flush. "Well it was quite lovely. But I feel we should head back. It's getting dark and I don't want to attempt anything with this shadow thing at night."

As they left, Tinkerbell hovered behind, her light flickering. Then a deep voice curled through the trees; a voice only she could hear.

"You endangered him."

Tinkerbell stiffened. She knew that voice: it was Death.

"I didn't mean—"

"You let your jealousy cloud your judgment. He is not yours to keep, Tinkerbell. You must grow, or suffer the consequences."

Tinkerbell swallowed hard. She had never feared Death before, but his words carried a weight that made her wings falter.

That night, as the treehouse slumbered, Tinkerbell perched on a high branch, gazing into the abyss of the Forbidden Forest. The whispers of the shadows still curled around the edges of her mind, teasing, taunting. She had wanted Wendy gone, but not like that.

Beneath her, Wendy stirred in her hammock. "Peter?"

Peter sat beside her; his silhouette outlined by the moonlight. "I'm here."

She hesitated, then softly asked, "When Sister Joy said you were dead, and that you sprinkled pixie dust on us to bring us here..I think I finally understand. But, Peter..if something happens to us here, what happens to our bodies back home?"

Peter exhaled, his voice quiet but firm. "If your soul's journey ends here, there is no going back."

A chill ran through Wendy, but she only nodded, her thoughts swirling with unspoken fears. "And if we stay?"

"If you stay here with me, you never grow up; never grow old."

"Never die too, because truthfully, if I stay here, I die there. I never get to grow up and grow old—fall in love. Have my baby boy..." Her voice trailed off as her mind lingered on the idea of her holding a baby in a blue blanket as her husband stood in the shadows of the hospital.

Up in the branches, Tinkerbell hugged her knees to her chest. For the first time, she wondered if she had gone too far. And worse— if Neverland itself was starting to change in ways she hadn't foreseen. To have not only the Heart Stone reach out to her but Death himself. Tinkerbell had better make things right..and soon.

HOURGLASS

The hospital ward was quieter than usual that evening. The dim glow of lanterns flickered against the aged walls, their light casting long shadows that stretched across the wooden floors. Sister Joy moved silently from bed to bed, adjusting blankets, murmuring quiet prayers, and checking on the children as they slept.

When she reached the supply closet at the end of the hall, she hesitated. A soft sound, barely more than a whisper, reached her ears—quiet sniffles, like a child crying.

With gentle hands, she pushed the door open. There, curled in the corner among neatly-stacked linens, was William. His small, ghostly frame shuddered as he wiped at his translucent face. When he looked up at her, his spectral eyes shimmered with sorrow.

"Come now, child," Sister Joy murmured, kneeling beside him. "Why are you hiding in the closet and crying? Shouldn't you be in bed?" she asked softly

William sniffled and rubbed his sleeve across his nose before looking up at her with an intensity that sent a chill down her spine. "Sister?"

"Yes, child?"

"You don't know? Maybe I should show you."

"Know what? Show me?"

Before she could respond, William's small hand shot out and grasped hers. A rush of cold spread through her bones as a sudden gust of energy whirled around them. A brilliant blue light shone forth, and the world blurred into an ethereal haze.

The closet was gone in an instant. The blue light danced in Sister Joy's vision, swirling like mist, and then—everything changed. They stood in a different hospital, miles away. The air felt heavy, thick with unspoken sorrow.

Sister Joy blinked as the world reassembled itself around her. The scent of antiseptic filled her nose, mixed with something metallic—was it blood? No, not quite. Something else.

She stood in a hallway, but it wasn't the one she knew. The walls were sterile white; the air thick with the quiet hum of an old hospital. A chill ran down her spine as she noticed a newspaper left on a nearby table. The date read *April 4, 1914.*

Her breath caught as she read the bold headline:

The U.S. Senate Votes to Declare War Against Germany, 82-6.

The paper was not yellowed or worn—it looked as if it had just come off the press. The realization settled in like a weight in her chest.

"William," she breathed. "Where are we?"

The little ghost stood beside her, his hand still holding hers. "I brought you here, Sister. This place, this time."

"But how? Why?"

William's small fingers trembled against her palm. He turned his head toward the long corridor ahead, where the faint sound of footsteps echoed toward them. "Because this is the day," he whispered.

"The day?" she pressed gently.

He swallowed hard. "The day my daddy lied to Mommy."

"How did he?"

William hesitated before speaking again, his small voice barely above a whisper. "This is the day my daddy lied to Mommy. Daddy said Momma was sick and he was going to give her a shot to make her all better. She went to sleep and never woke up. See?"

He pointed to a younger Dr. Anderson walking down the hallway, holding a child's hand. They passed right by Sister Joy and William without a glance.

"Sister, they can't see us. We can't do anything but watch," William explained as he led her toward a hospital bed. A pale woman lay upon it, her frail frame trembling as violent coughs racked her body.

"Momma," William whimpered, clutching her hand.

"Now, now, William. I need you to be a strong boy for Momma," she said weakly. "I am very sick—we both are."

"Momma, are you going to die?"

The woman's eyes shimmered with unshed tears, but she forced a smile. "Daddy is going to give Momma some medicine so I don't suffer. It will make me all better, little one. Oh, I love you, William."

I love you too, Momma. His tears blurred his vision as he clung to her fingers.

"Now, be a brave little man and go draw Mommy a picture. The nice nurse over there has paper and crayons for you."

William hesitated, but obeyed, shuffling over to a desk. Dr. Anderson knelt beside his wife; his face unreadable. "Anna."

"Andy, promise me something."

"Promise what?"

"Promise that when we die, whatever this is doesn't take us to a mass grave. Give us a proper burial. A proper funeral."

His jaw clenched. "My wife and son are not going to die."

"Andy, just promise me."

He sighed, nodding. "Fine. I promise."

Anna gave a small, relieved smile. "Good. My soul can be at peace."

"Anna..."

"Do it. My father has ensured you will be compensated. End this."

Dr. Anderson pulled a vial from his coat, his hands steady as he prepared the syringe. Sister Joy watched in horror as he pierced Anna's skin and delivered the mysterious pink solution into her vein. When it was done, he pocketed the syringe and turned toward William.

"William, come say goodbye to Mommy. We need to go."

"Bye, Mommy. I love you," William whispered, pressing one last kiss to her cooling cheek. Her eyelids fluttered shut, and her breathing slowed—then stopped.

Dr. Anderson's expression didn't change. "Come, William. We need to go to my lab."

"No!"

"Son, come with me. Now."

William shook his head furiously. "Daddy, I said no!"

Dr. Anderson knelt in front of him, voice soft. "Where is your sense of adventure, little man?" He reached into his coat again, retrieving a smaller syringe. In one swift motion, he plunged the needle into William's neck.

Sister Joy gasped as the boy's small body went limp in his father's arms. His breathing was shallow and rhythmic.

A nurse passing by stopped, her brow creased with concern. "Doctor, is young William alright?"

"Oh, I think he just overexerted himself," Dr. Anderson replied smoothly. "He wanted to see Anna, but he fell asleep. I'll take him to his bed in my lab. I think a good nap will do him just fine."

Rage and grief swirled inside Sister Joy as she stormed toward the doctor. Inches from his face, she screamed, "We will have you arrested for this!"

A rush of blue light surged around her, drowning out her fury. When the glow faded, she had stumbled back into the supply closet. Her breath came in short gasps and she clutched her chest, willing her heartbeat to slow. Tears of anger ran down her cheeks.

She glanced down at her watch. Only five minutes had passed.

Her mind reeled. She had just witnessed an entire morning unfold, yet time had barely moved.

"William?" she called out.

Silence. The ghostly child was gone once again.

SHADOW PLAY

The ward was eerily quiet as Dr. Anderson did his walking rounds, looking over all the children's charts. After reviewing charts and his notes, an evil grin danced across his face. He circled back around to a couple children, trying to decide which one would be his next candidate. His hands itched with excitement as he debated which child would receive the next micro-dose of toxic illness.

"Samantha here seems to have the body of a fighter. Well, we can't have you getting better so soon. Dear Mommy and Daddy can surely pay me more to keep you alive." Dr. Anderson briefly looked around then opened his white coat to check the vials attached inside. "According to your chart you have had many vaccines, so I need to see what else I can give you."

Samantha started to stir and gently mumble as she gained consciousness once more. Her skin was taking on a little color. Dr. Anderson pulled a vial of murky black fluid from the pocket inside his lap coat. He let out a cold dark chuckle, seeing the name of the specimen neatly printed on it.

"There is something I need to get off my chest. You are the same age as William when I gave him this very shot. Sadly, I have yet to create the cure to this. I sure hope your parents can afford to help fund my research."

Dr. Anderson looked up at the grandfather clock when it struck midnight. His attention was then directed to a shadow that danced across the wall. The short body was that of a child. Someone was awake and shouldn't be. On top of that, someone was out of bed and he was now in danger of being caught.

"Well, well, well, looks like someone else will get this shot. But I can't have you awake yet."

He pulled out a sedative and injected it into Samantha's saline iv bag. Once the solution was inside, Dr. Anderson shifted the bag to mix it fully. Out of the corner of his eye, once again he saw a shadow move across the room.

"Enough, little one. No need to hide. I'm a doctor and I'm here to help. So let's come out, shall we? Come out now." Dr. Anderson's patience was wearing thin.

The sound of little feet running across the cold marble floor echoed through the ward. Dr. Anderson's irritation started to boil over as he went from bed to bed, checking for a child that was far too awake.

Not finding what he was looking for, he started turning up all the oil lamps, illuminating every corner of the Rose Ward. When he turned the corner, he ran smack into the nurse.

"Dr. Anderson, can you explain why you are being so loud and turning on all the lamps? You know the hospital's policy. You are wasting valuable oil and resources. If you need my help, I will go on the bedside visits with you. But please allow the children to rest."

"Excuse me, Nurse?" Dr. Anderson shot out a dark unapproving glare.

"It's Nurse Holmes," she stated, adjusting her uniform.

"Well, Nurse Holmes, if I cared for a word you have to say, I'd ask you for it. As far as the resources go, I would not need to if you would keep a better eye on the children. I heard one of them out of bed. Now let me kindly remind you I am a doctor and you are…oh that is right, a nurse. So never get in my way again."

With that, Dr. Anderson shoved past her as he exited the Rose Ward. The nurse said behind him, "Excuse me. I wouldn't give a good God damn if you were the pope. If you bothered to know your patients, besides the size of their parents' bank accounts, you would know we don't have a single bed empty and none of these children are able to get out of bed."

Dr. Anderson rubbed his temples, the sterile glow of the overhead lamp doing little to ease the pounding in his skull. The long hours were getting to him, surely. But then why did the shadow in the corner seem to pulse with something more than mere darkness?

He exhaled sharply and turned his attention back to his notes. The serum was close—so close. If he could just refine the formula; push past these final limitations... He glanced up again. The shadow had deepened, stretching unnaturally across the wall. His pen stilled in his grip. The air thickened, charged with something unseen.

"Is it the long hours," he muttered, "or am I just going crazy?"

The oil lamps above flickered. A whisper—soft, unintelligible—drifted through the still air. His breath hitched. No one else was supposed to be in the office.

Dr. Anderson gathered the trash from his office and was heading down to the incinerator when he ran right into Sister Joy. His anger fell from his face as he took in her natural beauty. As he stood there before Sister Joy, his usual smug expression softened into something resembling charm—at least, that's what he thought.

"Sister Joy, a pleasure to see you tonight. I must say, your ivory skin looks exquisite under the moonlight."

Sister Joy barely concealed her shudder of disgust. Her sharp eyes flicked to the black trash bag in his grip. "What's in the bag, Doctor? And why are you hiding it here?"

Dr. Anderson chuckled, a deep, rumbling sound that carried more menace than mirth. "Well, Sister, what does one put in a black trash bag? I could show you—perhaps you'd like to accompany me to the incinerator? I hear the glow can be something...romantic."

Sister Joy snatched the bag from his hands without hesitation. Her fingers pressed into the plastic as she ripped it open. The scent of chemicals and rotting paper filled the air. Inside was nothing but discarded notes, empty vials, and broken syringes.

She exhaled sharply, then shoved the bag back at him with force. "Trash. Just like you."

Dr. Anderson caught the bag, his grip tightening as his charming facade shattered. His lips curled into a snarl, but before he could snap back, Sister Joy turned on her heels and strode away.

Anderson watched her go, fingers flexing as he resisted the urge to throw the bag against the wall. He inhaled through his nose, trying to rein in his irritation. He had no time for self-righteous women standing in his way—not tonight.

What had gotten into her? More importantly, what had gotten into Nurse Holmes?

His jaw clenched as he thought about their confrontation in the ward. Who was she to challenge him? A nurse—nothing more. And yet, she had dared to talk back; to insinuate that he didn't know his own patients. Worse, she had made a fool of him.

He stormed toward the incinerator, boots echoing down the dimly-lit hallway. His mind raced with anger, but underneath it all, a creeping unease slithered into his thoughts. The shadow. He had seen it move. It had been watching him. He shoved the thought aside. It was a trick of the light. A child's imagination. Nothing more. But as he reached the incinerator room, something was off. The air felt..heavier. The flickering light overhead buzzed louder than usual.

And then, as he pulled open the incinerator door, the shadows in the corner of the room seemed to shift. It was once again watching and waiting. "Get a grip," he hissed to himself. Yet the sense of being watched clung to him like a second skin.

As the fire grew from the deposit of the trash, the shadows shifted and danced on the walls, some seeming almost inhuman in nature. A cold weight settled on him, and once more he twisted his head up to the Rose Ward. "Oh Samantha, I have not forgotten about you. Fear not, I'm on my way. I already got your dear mommy and daddy to sign papers when we admitted you. Once you die, you belong to me forever. I will have to let William know he will be getting a sister of sorts."

There was a sudden crash in the next room, and Dr. Anderson twisted on the spot. Walking to the door way of the lab he discovered a beaker had fallen from the counter, its shattered remains glinting against the tile. His pulse thundered in his ears. Slowly, he pushed back his door, standing on unsteady legs.

He took a cautious step forward. The darkness in the corner seemed to writhe, shifting, stretching toward him. A figure? A presence? A faint glow emanated from within. Panic settled on his dark heart, fearing who might dare go into his lab and what they may find. The question that burned in his mind: *did he cover William's body?*

Nurse Holmes was found in the lab, her hands trembling, her eyes unfocused. Dr. Anderson stood there, his stomach twisting at the sight before him.

She was seated at the counter, a syringe in her hand. Blood dripped from the tip. Her arm was outstretched, veins swollen from repeated punctures, and yet she didn't seem to register the damage she was inflicting upon herself.

"Nurse Holmes," he said carefully, stepping forward. "What are you doing?"

She turned her head in a slow, mechanical motion. Her pupils were dilated, her skin pallid under the artificial light. "I heard you," she whispered. "You told me to do it. You said we needed more."

A chill ran down his spine. "I didn't—"

Her lips curled into something between a smile and a grimace. "Yes, you did."

His gaze flickered to the vials on the counter. All filled with her own blood. The sight was grotesque, unnatural.

A shadow passed over the room, a whisper brushing against the edge of his consciousness.

"More," it breathed.

Dr. Anderson's vision swam, his mind clawing against an unseen force pressing in. The presence was here. It had always been here.

Nurse Holmes let out a breathy giggle, her fingers tightening around the syringe. "We have to finish the work, Doctor."

Dr. Anderson pulled the syringe from her hand. As he applied pressure to stop the bleeding, she collapsed in his arms.

"Nurse Holmes, I don't know why you are here, but you stumbled into the spider's web. Why were you draining your blood so carelessly?"

"Because, Doctor, you asked me to donate life. Blood is life."

"When did I ask this of you?" Dr. Anderson's face scrunched up, confused as to what she was speaking about.

"After you took the trash out, I found you standing by Samantha's bedside. You told me you needed life for her. I asked how I could be of help, and you told me she needed a total blood transplant."

"You do know, that if you did that, well, you would be dead." Dr. Anderson looked at her eyes, now white and completely void of light. "Not to mention, I have not yet reached Samantha's bed again. Nurse Holmes, can you see me?"

"No, no I can't. One of the children's parents jumped out at me, trying to get my attention, and I got something in my eyes. I slowly lost my vision. Perhaps you can help me, Doctor." Nurse Holmes reached out to him, only to pull back again. "Dr. Anderson, I'm not a religious woman, but I must say something about you right now."

"What?" Dr. Anderson looked at her with a raised brow.

"Something tells me I should just go." Nurse Holmes stood up, attempting to find her way without vision.

"It's a shame, Nurse."

"What is, sir?"

"It's a shame you can't see."

"Oh, it will be all right. I 'm certain my vision will come back."

"That is what we're afraid of."

"We?"

"Why yes. This voice in my head is telling me you know too much. Now, you're not really what we would call an entrée; you're more like a simple snack."

"What? I am confused, sir."

"Say hello to my wife and son."

With that, the doctor gave her an injection. The last thing Nurse Holmes knew was the coldness of a needle pressed into her hip, and a burning sensation as the solution ate away at her veins. She soon dropped to the floor, as shadows crawled off of Dr. Anderson and swallowed her soul into oblivion. Leaving behind a dry empty husk.

"Well, that makes it easy. Nobody to worry about now." Dr. Anderson stepped over the shadow and walked back up the old stone steps to the Rose Ward. Once at the door, he dusted himself off as a shadow wrapped itself around him. He entered the ward to see a child's shadow dart off into the corner. With and evil glint in his eye, he began to sing a song—a children's rhyme.

"One, two," he hummed, "I am coming for you."

"Three, four," he jiggled his keys, "the doctor's at the door."

"Five, six, you better get in bed quick." He turned and locked the door with fire in his eyes, then he turned back to the ward.

"Seven, eight, now it's too late."

"Nine, ten, never see the daylight again."

Dr. Anderson looked over at the first child he could find with a glint in his eye, and stalked over to them like a predator to prey.

Dr. Jacobson was hard at work pouring over his medical journals, trying to find the common string that tied all of these children together. Suddenly, William appeared before him, catching him off guard.

"Hey, little man, what has you out of bed? It's almost one in the morning."

"The bad man. He's going to hurt them." William suddenly turned and ran to the Rose Ward.

"Sister Joy!" Dr. Jacobson yelled out, startling her. She jumped up and ran to his side.

"Yes, Dr. Jacobson. What is it?"

"Did you see a little boy?"

"Oh, you see him too." The sister put her hand over her mouth.

"I have questions, but they can wait. Did you see him run by? He was headed for Dr. Anderson's ward. He said the bad—"

"The bad man is going to hurt them." She finished the sentence. "Like hell on my watch!" she said and stormed off to the Rose Ward, hot on William's heals. Within seconds, she was at the locked door, shaking the handle urgently. "Nurse Holmes! Open up. It's Sister Joy. It's an emergency."

Hearing the noise at the door caused Dr. Anderson's head to snap and twist in an unnatural way. His eyes narrowed as he let out a hiss, and his body crumbled to the ground. As he went down, he hit his head on Nurse Holmes' desk.

Dr. Jacobson arrived at the door with a fireman's axe. "Sister, step aside," he said. In a matter of two hits, the door was broken, and they both found Dr. Anderson out cold on the floor. The only movement on the ward came from the curtains over the open window by the desk.

WALK WITH ME

Peter sat watching Wendy as she slept in the hammock, his eyes occasionally drifting to the Lost Boys. Finally, he looked up at Tinkerbell's house. The lights were on—she was home—but after everything that had happened today, he wasn't ready to face her.

The winds shifted and Peter suddenly sat up, his eyes wide as he looked for the unexpected visitor. "I know you're here, boss. I-I mean...I think that—" Peter was cut off with a firm hand on his shoulder.

"Peter. Peter. My sweet, innocent, and very gullible boy." Death let out a gentle sigh.

"So...you're not mad at me, Mr. Death?" Peter twisted anxiously under his grip.

"Peter, you're old enough." Death's gaze drifted to Wendy, his skeletal face softening in amusement. "Old enough to notice girls. She's quite pretty, isn't she?"

"Well yeah, if you're into that sort of thing. But girls are nothing but trouble. I see it all the time: kids grow up, fall in love, have kids..."

"That's called growing up, Peter."

"Yeah, but they have kids and die on them, leaving them alone in a world that never really wanted them, and then—" Peter's voice faltered. His eyes glistened as he fought back emotions, he rarely let surface.

"My boy, not everyone has the same fate you had. What happened to you was beyond my hand. I did not take your mother." Death's hand squeezed his shoulder.

"Why are you here?" Peter looked puzzled as he met Death's gaze. Death chuckled softly. "Peter, you are a typical boy—at your age, even in death you are clueless. I know you like Wendy, and that's okay. I just need you to be fair to her. Keeping her here prevents her from growing up. You heard her tell you she wants to hold a baby in her arms one day...Peter, you can't give her that."

Peter swallowed hard but said nothing as he watched Wendy breathe so peacefully. The gentle movement of her eyes told him she was dreaming. "Now that one..." Death pointed his boney hand to Tinkerbell's house. "I made her for you."

"Tink is my friend. I don't see her like that..."

"Oh, so you admit you have feelings for Wendy? Maybe it was the kiss that sealed the deal."

"You saw that?" Peter's face turned red.

Death laughed. "Of course I did. Peter, its fine, but please don't go breaking her heart for a boy she can never have. Now, as far as Tinkerbell goes—no, she was not made to be your girlfriend. But she is a being that has her own autonomy. She has fallen for you and became Jealous. I have already spoken to her—that's why she is afraid to come down."

Peter looked away, his stomach twisting with guilt.

"Peter, I want you to walk with me. I have some souls to collect and this will give you time to think."

"Yes Death." Peter hesitated, then placed his hand in Death's, as the world around them faded into darkness.

When Peter opened his eyes again, they were walking in the shadows of a small town. A run-down shack loomed before them, its dimly-lit interior revealing an elderly couple whispering their final goodbyes

"Betty," the old man murmured, his smile faint but tender. "I still have the letter you left me on that old oak stump sixty-two years ago."

The frail woman gazed into his eyes, a loving glint shining through her weariness. "I remember every word I wrote in that note. William, I may be old and dying, but I'm not dead yet."

"Stop that death talk." William bit back tears. "Because I need you to hear me out. In your note, you told me that if you get there before I do..." His voice caught in his throat.

"I know Billy, I won't give up on you. On us. We've had some amazing years of adventure. I know you will meet me when your time is through. The Lord calls us home, and we know not the day nor the hour. Darlin', just meet me inside the middle east gate." Betty placed her hand on her husband's face one last time before she faded from this world.

Death stepped forward and extended his hand. Her soul, now young and radiant, emerged from her withered body. She wiped a tear from her face, looking at her husband crying over her body. She took Death's hand, and ascended the ethereal staircase that had appeared before them.

Peter's throat tightened. "Death..."

"Peter," Death said gently, "it's not the goodbyes that hurt. It's the flashbacks that follow. They ripple like tears in an endless pool."

"Flashbacks?" Peter scrunched his eyebrows together.

"Yes. Those moments of bliss—even the painful ones. They have a way of cutting deeper than the farewell itself."

"Why would anyone want that?" Peter watched as William sat silently by his wife's bedside, his eyes distant. He wasn't just staring—he was reliving.

"Right now," Death continued, "he's remembering the first time he met Betty—the way she walloped him on the head for pulling her pigtails. He's remembering the first time he tried to kiss her, the meals he cooked for her; the time he made her cry on her nineteenth birthday. The human mind is fragile, Peter. We may forget words or voices, but we never forget how someone made us feel."

"Death, why are you showing me this?" Peter started to feel the man's raw emotions, and it was causing his own eyes to flood with tears.

"Because I don't want you to rob Wendy of her Billy. Maybe in another time, another place, another lifetime—your souls will meet again. But Peter, you are an agent of death. Life cannot exist without death, but we cannot take what is not ours."

Peter swallowed hard. "I only brought them to protect them from that crazy doctor."

"I know, Peter." Death turned; his hollow gaze fixed on the horizon. Something dark loomed beyond the veil of the mortal world. "Things are not well. Forces from our realm are crossing over."

Peter tensed. "What do you need me to do?"

"Peter, I need you to promise me, that when the time comes, you will let Wendy go. Let the Lost Boys go."

"Yes sir."

"Good boy. Now, I must ask you to go back and get Tinkerbell. Something is off. Strange forces ancient powers are here now, and I need to get to the bottom of it. Peter, I need you to work. Save and cross over as many lost boys and girls as you can. When you save a light in this world, it gives you strength, because they are with you even after they cross over. The Shadow is growing hungry." Death's expression darkened. "Hook was meant to collect only the wicked, and lost souls but the Shadow craves the souls of children. You cannot let them win."

Peter clenched his fists. "Then we fight."

Death nodded. "Then we fight."

"What about all the souls Hook is taking?"

155

"His soul needs some serious redemption. The Beast is his master. He is to only collect dark souls like his own. Ones that make deals and fail to pay the price. But I know the Shadow has a hunger for the souls of children. They are pure, they have more power to them. You cannot let them win."

"No child needs to be swallowed for all eternity by that thing." Peter shivered as he looked over his shoulder and nodded to the hospital. "Death, that Dr. Anderson, something is not right with that man."

"Peter, we don't get to pick and choose our ancestry. It seems to me that rotten to the core runs in his family. But I need you to return to Neverland and tell Tinkerbell I need her to focus and help you. Peter Pan, I am counting on you."

With that, Death faded away, leaving Peter to watch as the old man picked up the phone to call the authorities and report his wife finally passing.

THE CAPTAIN'S BARGAIN

The air in Neverland was thick with the scent of salt and earth, a mixture of the sea breeze rolling in from the coast and the rich aroma of the island's untamed greenery. The moon hung low, casting silver beams through the dense canopy of ancient trees, their leaves whispering with the stories of the past. Fireflies blinked lazily between the thick vines, and somewhere in the distance, the faint, eerie laughter of mermaids drifted up from the hidden lagoons.

Peter walked with careful steps, the soft moss beneath his boots muffling his movements. Every so often, the calls of night creatures punctuated the silence—a distant wolf-like howl, the rustling of unseen wings, the murmur of forgotten spirits that had long made this place their home. Neverland had always felt alive, but now, it felt heavier, as if the island itself knew the weight of the task Peter carried.

"Come on, Tink. We need to talk," Peter said, his voice gentle but firm.

Tinkerbell hesitated, casting a faint golden glow over the brim of his hat as she settled there, her wings occasionally flicking as though she, too, felt the energy that pulsed beneath their feet. The night sounds around them only deepened the emotions.

Peter was the first to break the silence. "Tink…I like you. But not like-like," he admitted, glancing up at her perched form. "You're my best friend. That's something that means the world to me. But it's not…the way you wanted."

Tinkerbell was quiet for a long moment, then she let out a soft sigh, inhaling shakily before saying, "I thought maybe…maybe you…just didn't know yet. That one day, you'd see me differently."

Peter smiled slightly. "You're too important to me to lie, Tink. I'd rather have you as my best friend forever than risk losing you over something that was never meant to be."

She nodded, wings shimmering in the moonlight. "Different, but still together?"

Peter grinned. "Always."

Tinkerbell gave a small, relieved laugh before her expression turned serious again. "Peter...I'm sorry."

He glanced at her, his expression unreadable. "I know. I spoke with Death. We have a mission."

"You don't have to do this alone, Peter," Tinkerbell said softly, the usual mischief in her voice absent.

Peter exhaled. "I do."

She hovered closer, her tiny fists clenched. "But what if—"

"No." His tone was gentle but firm. "You'll always be my friend, Tink. But this...this is my burden."

She lowered her gaze, her wings fluttering uncertainly. Peter reached out, his finger brushing against her tiny hand. She didn't pull away, but the distance between them had never felt greater.

Just then, a shadow loomed over them, and the moment shattered.

Hook was standing on the shore, his coat billowing like a specter of his former self. His eyes, dark as the abyss beneath his ship, held an emotion Peter couldn't quite name.

"You think this is a game, boy?" Hook's voice was a blade honed on years of bitterness. "My crew and I answer to and older power."

Peter didn't flinch. "You sold your soul, Hook. And now you want to drag them down with you."

Hook's jaw tightened. "You know nothing of sacrifice. In life deals are made every day. There is a price to everything my boy. The crew knew that when I started collecting them."

He took a step forward, the sand swallowing his boots. "I did what I had to do. The darkness doesn't just take—it demands. A price must be paid, or it will claim all of Neverland. Would you rather the entire island be consumed? Boy, give it what it wants and it may spare those precious lost boys of yours."

Peter hesitated. There was something raw in Hook's words, a flicker of pain beyond his usual venom. "Is that what you tell yourself?"

Hook's lips curled, but it wasn't quite a sneer. "I tell myself the truth. Unlike you, I see the bigger picture. One of the gifts of being an adult."

Tinkerbell darted between them, her glow flaring hot. "You don't get to make that choice for them!" she snapped, but there was an undertone— something wounded, something personal. Hook had always treated her differently, not with kindness, but with acknowledgment, as though she mattered more than the rest. And now? Now he was throwing it all away, just like he always did.

Hook barely spared her a glance. "Stay out of this, pixie."

"Don't talk to Tinkerbell like that!" Peter's hand rested on his small dagger.

Tinkerbell, emboldened by frustration, hovered closer. "Why are you hunting children's souls, Hook?"

The pirate sighed, something heavy in his demeanor. "I made a deal. A devil's bargain. My bloodline is cursed, and this…this is my penance. I have to cull the souls of the lost. I believed I was saving future generations. But the darkness is never full, it is always hungry. Although through the years I did discover its taste for the souls of the young."

Tinkerbell's wings fluttered furiously. "You think stealing children's souls is saving them? How can you justify that?"

Hook clenched his jaw. "I don't expect you to understand, fairy. I was not always culling children's souls." But then he hesitated, the weight of his actions pressing on him. Seeing the pain in Tinkerbells eyes, "Search my cargo hold. Before it comes back."

"Before who comes back?" Peter met Hook's cold gaze.

"The Shadow," was all Hook managed to say before he turned away. Peter and Tinkerbell exchanged a look before rushing below deck.

Their breath caught as they found dozens of children huddled together, frightened but unharmed. Some whimpered at the sight of Peter, their eyes wide with fear and uncertainty. Others shrank into the shadows, their small bodies trembling. The air was thick with the scent of damp wood and desperation.

A little girl clung to an older boy, her tiny hands gripping his torn sleeve as if he was the only thing keeping her safe. Her wide eyes shimmered with unshed tears. "Is he going to take us again?" she whispered.

The older boy, his face smudged with dirt, shook his head. "No. Not this time."

One boy, no older than five, reached out and clung to Peter's sleeve, his voice a trembling whisper. "Please.. don't let him take us."

Peter's heart clenched, his fists balling at his sides. "I won't. I promise."

More children slowly emerged from the shadows, their faces gaunt, their eyes hollow with exhaustion. Some of them had been here longer than others, and it showed. They didn't know whether to trust Peter, but hope flickered in their expressions like a dying ember.

Quickly they opened the cages freeing the children. When they returned topside, Peter's glare could have burned through steel. Peter looked at Hook and demanded, "Why the sudden change of heart?"

Hook exhaled deeply. "The Shadow is hunting two child's soul in particular—a boy named William, the other I am unsure of. I don't know why, but something about it... it sits poorly with my soul."

For a moment, Hook seemed lost in thought, his gaze distant; haunted. The moonlight caught the gleam of his steel hook, and his coat, rich with the scent of sea salt and something darker, swayed with the night breeze. There was an old sorrow in his eyes, one he refused to name. Perhaps there had been a boy once—someone he had lost. Someone he had failed.

Peter took a step forward, his expression set. "I won't let you take them."

160

Hook's voice turned grave as he met Peter's eyes. "I know we're not on the same side, boy, but this—this is right." Putting his hands up in mock surrender. "But make no mistake, if you bring harm to them, I *will* come for you."

Tinkerbell darted forward. "Hook, stop! Peter did nothing wrong. This was *my* fault."

Hook's expression softened slightly, but only for her. He reached into his coat and withdrew a small, ornate flute, pressing it into Peter's hand.

Peter hesitated before taking it. The instant his fingers wrapped around the instrument, a strange sensation coursed through him—like a whisper brushing against his ears, distant and sorrowful. A faint, eerie wail drifted at the edge of his hearing, gone as quickly as it came. The flute was unnervingly cold, like it had been carved from the breath of ghosts. His grip tightened, his instincts screaming that this was no ordinary artifact.

Peter turned it over, frowning. "What is this?"

Hook's fingers lingered on the instrument for a fraction longer than necessary, his voice lower, rougher. "Play it anywhere children have died. If their souls remain trapped, it will call them to you." His gaze darkened. "This was given to me once, long ago. I never had the heart to use it." Peter swallowed, nodding.

Hook's lips curled into a smirk, but his eyes were serious. "Know this, boy. I do this for her, not for you. But if you ever make Tinkerbell cry again..." His grin widened dangerously. "I'll gut you like a codfish."

"Peter, let's get out of here. We can help the children once we're safe in our part of the island." Tinkerbell's wings fluttered rapidly in anticipation of what might be coming back.

"Listen to your little fairy, boy. I don't know how long my master and the crew will be gone. Just keep the flute safe—you will know when you need to use it."

Hook tipped his cap, turning away from the children as Peter instructed Tinkerbell.

"Tink, sprinkle them with pixie dust."

Peter stood in front of the children. "I need all of you to believe. Believe in me. She will sprinkle you with pixie dust. Take each other's hands and think happy thoughts."

He turned to see one of the older children, a boy no older than twelve, gripping the hand of a younger one. "What if staying means we survive?"

Peter crouched to their level. "I know it's scary," he admitted. "But you have to trust me. Believe that there's something better than this."

The boy swallowed hard, uncertainty flickering across his face—until the younger child squeezed his hand and whispered, "I believe in Peter Pan."

The older boy exhaled, the tension in his shoulders easing. "Okay," he whispered. "Okay."

Peter straightened and turned back to Hook. "This is where it ends."

Hook's gaze flickered to the children, something unreadable passing through his eyes. Then, with a bitter chuckle, he stepped back toward the water. "Foolish boy," he murmured, as the inky waves lapped at his heels.

The *Jolly Roger*, once a proud fortress, groaned as the shadows curled around it. It wasn't sinking—it was being consumed. The darkness pulled it down, piece by piece, until only the torn sails remained above the surface.

Hook met Peter's eyes one last time. "You'll see," he said, his voice almost soft. "One day, you'll see." And then he was gone.

A voice trembled behind him. "What if he's right?"

Peter stood still, the weight of the moment pressing against him. He glanced at Tinkerbell, who hovered beside him, her expression unreadable.

"Come on," he said finally. "We have a journey ahead."

And as the children took their first steps toward a new beginning, the fireflies continued their dance, unaware of the battle that had just been fought in the heart of Neverland.

With that, Peter grabbed one child's hand. Soon, they were all linking hands, and Peter pushed off, taking them into the sky.

Looking back, Peter watched Hook take his ship out to sea, watching it sail away until it slipped below the waves.

THE BODY

Dr. Jacobson didn't realize why his heart raced as he pressed two fingers to Dr. Anderson's throat, searching for a pulse. Faint but steady. He was alive. Sister Joy exhaled in relief, clutching her rosary as she knelt beside the unconscious doctor. The dim light of the infirmary flickered, casting long shadows along the walls.

It was there, in the stillness of the night, that Dr. Jacobson started to think. He allowed his mind to open, and in that moment, he chose to ask what was on his mind. "Sister, we both saw a young boy but I know no child with the name William." Dr Jacobson looked at the nun with a puzzled expression.

"Dr., I know your faith has been called into question over the years, but while I have worked with you, I have grown accustom to seeing and hearing things that cannot be explained." Sister Joy looked around to make sure they were alone.

"Check his coat," Dr. Jacobson said, nudging the folded lapel of Dr.

Anderson's coat with his gloved hand.

Sister Joy hesitated, before slipping her hand into the deep pockets. Her fingers brushed against cold glass, and one by one, she pulled out syringes filled with mysterious, swirling liquids.

"Doctor, look," she whispered, holding up the vials.

Dr. Jacobson's expression darkened. He took one, turning it against the light. The viscous fluid inside shimmered oddly, catching unnatural hues. "I don't know what this is," he admitted, "but something about it doesn't look right."

Sister Joy nodded. "What should we do?"

"Well, first, we tie him up," Dr. Jacobson said. "Then, we call law enforcement. Also, Sister, we need to find the nurse and check on the children. I don't know what it is, but the Rose Ward feels very dark compared to our unit."

They bound Dr. Anderson's hands and feet with restraints from the infirmary, making sure he wouldn't be able to escape when he woke. Satisfied, they left him secured on the gurney and continued their rounds.

The corridors of the hospital were eerily silent as they made their way back the Darlings' room. Dr. Jacobson was about to push the door open, when a soft rustling behind them made him pause. He turned sharply, but the hall remained empty.

Then, an urgent voice whispered, "They are not safe. None of us are."

Dr. Jacobson and Sister Joy spun around. Standing just outside the dim reach of the oil light was William. His pale face was lined with fear; his eyes wide and haunted.

"William?" Sister Joy took a cautious step forward. "What do you mean?"

His lips trembled. "Daddy is coming. He broke free and you need to run" A chill ran down Dr. Jacobson's spine. "Who is your father?"

William's gaze darted past them toward the Rose Ward infirmary. His voice dropped to a whisper. "I believe you know it's Dr. Anderson. He abandoned me and Mommy."

Before they could ask anything more, William vanished into the darkness.

There was a loud bang and groan, and a moment later, Dr. Anderson came storming down the hall, pulling the restraints off his body as he ran. As soon as he got within reach, Dr. Jacobson grabbed him and slammed him into the wall, his eyes ablaze. He balled up his fist and punched Dr. Anderson in the face.

Sister Joy said, weeping, "How can you call yourself a doctor? How could you do that to your own son?"

"How could I abandon my son?" Dr. Anderson's voice, hoarse yet filled with eerie amusement, drifted through the infirmary. He stirred against the remaining remnants of his restraints, a slow, menacing smile spreading across his lips. "Simple."

Dr. Jacobson and Sister Joy stiffened, watching as he cracked open one puffy and swollen eye.

"I never loved his mother," Dr. Anderson continued, his voice devoid of remorse. "Love is such a waste. My only love is money. Lots and lots of money. The men in my family have no love for extra baggage. We have always only wanted fame and fortune. You think I am dark and twisted, Sister; I can tell by the look on your face that I disgust you."

A presence loomed in the shadows beyond him, as William stood there, silent, watching.

"Daddy? You never loved me or Mommy!" William's voice was frail like glass. "You lied to Mommy and you broke your promise."

"Sister?" Dr. Jacobson looked at Sister Joy with a puzzled expression, then turned back to the boy he saw moments before.

"Doctor, I believe the good Lord is allowing us to see what we need to see—to see beyond. Sister Agnus spoke of such a blessing. A gift as it were—to know that a soul trusts you enough to visit you and share knowledge that you might need at the time. Or even for them to say their goodbyes." Sister Joy pulled out a tissue and brushed away tears.

"You little shit. I thought it would have collected your worthless soul by now. It promised me wealth beyond my wildest dreams." Dr. Anderson looked out of his one good eye to see the ghost of his son. "It's a shame. Maybe if he would have collected you sooner, I might not have gotten caught. All well when he does come to collect you, maybe he can take them like he did that worthless nurse."

"I find it hard to believe you could ever have had a redeemable quality." Sister Joy looked at the ground then back to William. "Child, what did this bastard for a man promise you and your mother?"

"A proper funeral." William gritted his teeth.

"Ah, without it, you soul can't be a peace." Sister Joy picked up a bible.

"That won't help him; I sold his soul the day he was born." Dr. Anderson grinned, a sinister glint in his eye.

"This book *can* help him. William, do you know that death is not permanent? You can move on from this world into the next. I believe that we even have a chance to come back one day."

"What if we don't want to come back?" William looked around, seeing all the sickness in the ward. "What if I am done with this world—if it's filled with people like him."

"William, is it? Can you tell us where your body is located?" Dr. Jacobson inquired while sitting himself on the floor.

"What do you want with my body? Are you going to experiment on it like Daddy did?" William walked up to his father who was sitting on the floor. Squatting down to meet him at eye-level, he said, "I hate you."

"William, we want to ensure you get a proper funeral. Please, where is your body?" Dr. Jacobson pleaded.

"William, you can trust Dr. Jacobson and I." Sister Joy set her bible down, reaching out and taking hold of the child's spectral hands. "I know your mother is waiting for you. If you were my son, I would be waiting at the gates of Heaven every day for you."

"Oh, Heaven this, Heaven that. William, when the Shadow comes for you, and it will; go with it, don't fight it. I fathered you, and I am sure I have fathered other children that I don't even know about, just like many men before me have done. So you see, sacrificing you for wealth and power; I didn't think twice. Besides, I am only following in family tradition."

William pulled his hand back from Sister Joy and was ready to slap Dr. Anderson, when he suddenly gave up, knowing he could not physically hurt his own father.

"Follow me to the basement, but first lock him in a closet so he can't hurt any more children." William faded out of view, leaving Dr. Jacobson and Sister Joy to debate whether to follow him or not.

A faint shimmer filled the air, and Peter and Tinkerbell materialized at the door of the room, their presence bringing a momentary warmth to the overwhelming darkness.

Peter reached into his pocket and pulled out his flute.

"It's you! You came for me!" William screamed.

Peter stopped and crouched down, looking deep into the boy's eyes. "William?"

"I won't go! I won't go!" William screamed, causing Peter to back up from the boy.

"Tink, do something," Peter pleaded.

Tinkerbell flew out of Peter's hat and sat on William's noise, her wings flexing and shining in the night's light. "William, this is Peter Pan. He is here for all the lost boys and girls."

"No, he is the Shadow my daddy sold my soul to," exclaimed William, causing Peter to take another step back.

"William, I have been looking for you," Tinkerbell pleaded. William pulled back and looked up.

"Are you the Shadow?"

"The Shadow is an evil beast. It is exactly that: a shadow. It is obviously dark and evil, whereas you can see the light we give off. We have been sent here many times to cross over children, but most times we don't manage to find who we're looking for."

Lifting the flute to his lips, Peter set the first note free. A peaceful melody rang out; the air stirring with magic. Wisps of light began to appear— small, flickering figures forming in the heavy silence.

The children's souls gathered, drawn to the melody.

Suddenly, William ran into Peter's open arms. "Promise me— no promise us—that you're a nice guy."

"Oh little buddy, you remind me of so many of the lost boys. Now, gather round; we don't have much time. I am sure the Shadow is on its way. Lucky for us, it cannot survive long on its own in this world. It needs a host to hold on to." Peter gently ruffled William's hair.

"Oh, that would be my daddy, but the good doctor and sister have him tied up right now." William had a grin on his face, but it soon fell away.

"What's wrong, bud?" Peter lifted his face to meet William's.

"I sent them down here; down to where Daddy hides all of our bodies until he puts them in the big furnace." William pointed to the incinerator.

A sound at the door stopped them all in their tracks. It was Dr. Jacobson. The children wanted to run and hide, but the magic of the flute bound them to the room. The sound of a key in a lock weighed heavily on all of them as they stood frozen in fear.

It was the smell that hit them first: a pungent mix of decay and something metallic. Dr. Jacobson's stomach twisted as he stepped into the next room: Dr. Anderson's laboratory.

The horror made Sister Joy stagger back. Scattered across the cold tiles were bodies. Small, lifeless forms. The remains of over two-dozen children. Some whole, others…

Sister Joy choked back a sob, pressing a hand to her mouth.

Dr. Jacobson swallowed hard and reached for the nearest phone. "We need the police. Now."

Sister Joy closed her eyes, whispering a prayer. "Lord, I know You sent little Peter to bless us with his light. I only pray You give these children the same love and closure." With trembling hands, she reached for the door and shut it gently to preserve the scene.

"Wait, they didn't see us?" William questioned.

Tink replied, "No, I used my pixie magic to take the gift of true sight from them for now. But Peter, we must not stay long."

"I know, Tink. I Know." Peter looked out at the vast crowd of children. There were far more souls than bodies in the lab. "How long has he been doing this?" Peter muttered, half to himself.

"Those that came before me told me it was long before I joined. Sadly, our numbers dip because the Shadow catches us from time to time. With each one it takes, Daddy gets stronger," William explained while taking Peter by the hand. "I trust you," he said.

"We trust you," the other children said in unison.

"Tinkerbell, you know what we have to do now. It's faith, trust, and a sprinkling of..." Peter's voice trailed off.

"Pixie dust," Tinkerbell finished for him, fluttering her wings and tossing her magic dust over the children. "They are all yours, Peter."

CROSSING OVER

The children soared through the sky, laughter and excitement filling the crisp night air. Below them, the city shimmered with golden lights, though it was a place none of them had ever truly called home. The burden of pain and fear faded as their souls embraced the wind, rising higher with each breath.

"Look, I'm flying!" a child no older than five exclaimed, his tiny hands stretching toward the stars.

"Remember, kiddos, happy thoughts...and don't forget to hold hands. I don't want to lose anyone," Peter's voice called over the wind. He turned to his left, meeting the wide-eyed gaze of William, who clutched his hand tightly. Peter grinned. "All right, second star to the right and straight on till morning. Cock-a-doodle-doo!"

The children mimicked his call, their voices ringing with joy as they crowed into the night. Tinkerbell zipped between them, her tiny form leaving trails of golden pixie dust to ensure no child drifted away. When their feet finally touched solid ground, Neverland welcomed them home. The trees rustled as if whispering greetings, and glowing fireflies danced around them. Then, from the dense foliage, figures emerged.

"Peter's back!" the Lost Boys cheered, rushing forward in excitement.

Wendy stepped through the gathering with a knowing smile. "Off on another adventure, Peter?" she teased.

Before he could respond, they were rushed with all the usual questions:

"Where do we sleep?"

"Are there really mermaids?"

"Do pirates eat children?"

Peter laughed, holding up his hands to quiet them. "One at a time, you lot."

A young man with tousled dark hair stepped forward, a mischievous twinkle in his eye. "Hi, I'm Tobey, a Lost Boy from Neverland. Welcome to your wildest fantasy." With a dramatic flourish, he pulled a bouquet of flowers from thin air and bowed.

A small girl in a pink dress popped her thumb from her mouth long enough to ask, "What do you guys do all day?"

"Simple, we hang out with Peter Pan. There's always a new adventure on the horizon."

"What if I don't want adventure?"

Tobey smirked. "We hang out with Peter Pan and go on adventures."

"What if I don't want an adventure?" another child asked hesitantly.

"Well then we can play in the woods; swim in the lagoon with mermaids—" Tobey extended his hand.

Peter cut him off with a knowing look. "Not so fast, Tobey. I know you're excited to have someone new to beat at games, but trickery isn't our way. Who leads by tricks?"

"Hook," the children responded in unison.

Peter's expression softened as he turned to William. "There was a time when I was alone too, but a sister took me in and gave me grace." His voice wavered as vivid images of Sister Agnus filled his mind.

"You mean Sister Agnus, or Sister Joy?" William asked, squeezing Peter's hand.

Peter's smile returned. "Both."

"Where did you come from, Peter?" the little girl in pink pressed, her thumb sneaking back into her mouth.

Peter floated onto a tree stump at the heart of the gathering. "Nowhere, really. Just an ordinary boy with no place to call home."

Wendy rolled her eyes, chastising him playfully. "Oh, come on, Peter. You have a story. You have a home. Neverland is your home away from home."

Peter's gaze drifted to the stars. "I had no home. I was an orphan. The sisters raised me like a son, but I had no real family. My only friends were the ones I found in old storybooks."

"Peter, why did we die?" A small boy in a tattered hospital gown whispered the question like a secret.

Peter hesitated before crouching to the boy's level. "That's a story I haven't read yet," he admitted. "Sometimes, it's just our time. Other times...people like Dr. Anderson play a role in it." He gestured toward the sea of children.

"How did you die, Peter?" William asked as he held on to his other hand.

Peter took a deep breath. "The night I died, I already knew my time was up. When I closed my eyes, I felt him close." His voice softened, as if recalling an old lullaby. "He had the warmest heart, the kindest smile."

"Who?" Wyatt, the boy in the hospital gown, asked.

"Death." Peter let the word settle before continuing. "He spoke to me like an old friend, and he gave me a choice: I could either cross over, or stay and help others find their way. I chose to stay. He promised I would never be lonely; that I would always have a friend." Peter glanced at the tiny glowing figure beside him. "And he was right."

Silence stretched over the group until Wyatt broke it. "Wait, we had a choice?" His eyes filled with desperate hope. "Does that mean we can go back?"

William sighed, placing a gentle hand on Wyatt's shoulder. "Go back to what? Your body has long turned to ash," he said with a heavy heart. "We all saw the night my daddy was afraid of getting caught. He took all the bodies he had and burned them all to dust."

"Oh my, that sounds dreadful." Tinkerbell fluttered to her pedestal.

Tears welled in Wyatt's eyes as he looked at the others. "So this is it?"

Peter nodded. "This is Neverland. Here, Lost Boys like us are free to believe. To never grow up. To never die. I have become a junior reaper since that day. I am here to help you with your options. My job is to help children cross over. It is easy and it does not hurt. Or you can choose to stay here."

The children exchanged glances, some filled with wonder, others with quiet acceptance.

Then Tinkerbell, arms crossed, tapped her foot impatiently. "Peter, you're forgetting one thing…"

Peter arched a brow. "What's that, Tink?"

She huffed. "You forgot to tell them about the pirates."

"Yes, I must warn you—Neverland is not always safe," Peter said, his voice low and serious. "There is a pirate here, a reaper like me. But unlike me..he is not always a nice guy. He has a crew of lost souls. They are always on the hunt for those who are lost."

William perked up; his eyes wide with curiosity. "You guys always seem to be on the run from Captain Hook," he said, as Wendy leaned in to whisper something in his ear.

Before Peter could respond, a chilling voice echoed through the trees. "Run, run, Lost Boys, I say to thee." Suddenly, Captain Hook stepped out of the shadows, his presence sending a ripple of alarm through the Lost Boys. The flickering light of the fire cast long, eerie shadows across his face, making his expression unreadable.

Peter squared his shoulders and stepped forward; his gaze locked onto Hook's. "We've run for long enough, both from reality, and from you, Hook."

Tinkerbell flitted beside Peter, her tiny foot tapping impatiently in the air. "Peter," she started, but he held up a hand.

"Neverland is our home," Peter said, his voice steady. He turned to William. "This place is for Lost Boys like me and you. Here, we are free to believe. Here, we never have to grow up..never die."

Hook let out a deep sigh, the weight of something old and heavy settling onto his shoulders. "He's right, my boy," he said, kneeling before William. "Neverland is home to many. Here, you are safe."

Peter's grip tightened around his dagger, suspicion flaring in his eyes. "Hook, what are you playing at?"

Hook met Peter's gaze, and for the first time in a long time, there was something different—something raw.

"You have his eyes," Peter whispered, his dagger slipping from his fingers as he stepped closer. His hands gripped Hook's shoulders, searching his face.

Hook nodded slowly. "Peter...thank you for saving this little one." Peter's expression darkened.

"So you can take him?" His jaw clenched, his teeth gritting together.

Tinkerbell darted between them, glowing furiously. "Peter!" she snapped.

Hook raised a hand, a silent plea for calm. "It's okay, Tinkerbell." He took a slow breath, then removed his captain's hat and bowed his head. "I came here to ask you a favor, Peter."

Peter narrowed his eyes, stepping protectively in front of William. "What favor?"

Hook lifted his head, his voice unusually solemn. "That boy," he said, nodding toward William. "He is one of my own. My bloodline. If I had to name it, I suppose...I'd say I'm his grandfather. From over a hundred years back." The air around them grew colder, the weight of Hook's words settling over the group. Even the Lost Boys, usually fidgeting and restless, had gone still.

Hook's gaze darkened. "The Shadow has been feeding off the souls of my descendants because of my original sin—the deal I made long ago. It approaches each one of my line, whispering temptations, binding them with its curse. My latest grandson...he sold his own unborn son's soul." His voice wavered, thick with regret. "He sold William's soul."

Peter sucked in a sharp breath.

Hook clenched his fists. "It's not fair. William never asked for this fate. His father had no right to bargain with something that was never his to give." He looked at Peter with something that might have been desperation. "I want you to cross him over, Peter. Please. Give back to him what was stolen."

Silence hung between them, the weight of the request pressing into Peter's chest.

Tinkerbell hovered close, her glow dimming. "Peter..." she whispered.

Peter exhaled slowly, his eyes flicking to William—innocent, lost, and utterly unaware of the dark fate that loomed over him.

His fingers twitched at his side, his hand dancing across the flute. The Shadow was watching. Waiting. Hungry to claim what it felt was owed. And Peter had a choice to make.

Peter inhaled sharply, his fingers curling into fists at his sides. His eyes flicked to William, wide-eyed and innocent, standing on the edge of a fate he never chose.

For a long moment, Peter said nothing, as the wind whispered through the trees, carrying the weight of Hook's plea through the night. The Lost Boys shifted uneasily. Even Tinkerbell, usually quick to speak her mind, hovered silently, her glow dim and uncertain.

Then, Peter looked at Hook, his jaw set, his voice steady. "No." Hook flinched, but Peter wasn't finished. "I'm not just going to cross him over like he's some lost thing to be sent away."

Peter stepped closer; his expression fierce. "William is not a bargain. He is not a mistake. He is not yours to mourn or the Shadow's to claim."

Peter turned to William, his voice softening. "You deserve better than this." He reached out, pressing a hand against the boy's chest, where a faint, eerie pulse of darkness flickered beneath his skin.

Peter's eyes burned with determination as he turned back to Hook. "I won't just set him free; I'll break the Shadow's hold. I'll undo what your bloodline started." His gaze darkened, his voice dropping to a near growl. "And then I'm coming for *it*."

The air around them seemed to crackle, as if Neverland itself was listening.

Hook exhaled, his face unreadable, but there was something like relief in his eyes. "Then do what I never could, Peter."

Peter knelt in front of William, locking eyes with him. "Are you ready?"

William hesitated, then nodded.

Peter closed his eyes, drawing a slow breath. And as the winds of Neverland stirred around them, carrying whispers of forgotten souls, Peter Pan reached deep into the magic that bound the island, and for the first time, he did not just guide a child to Neverland, he brought a soul home.

Peter sat on the tree stump and pulled out the flute, pushing his own magic into the song. The Heart Stone came to life, pulsating a blue rhythmic wave that covered all of Neverland. Each wave that washed over William, the darkness grew less, until there was nothing left but the clean pure soul of a child.

Peter extended his hand while holding onto William, and a brilliant staircase appeared. "William, this set of stairs will lead you to a place where your heart will be very happy. I know you have someone waiting for you. I cannot hold you here, and I cannot force you up those stairs. The choice is always yours."

"Eh, Peter, who would be waiting for me?"

A woman's voice flowed down the stairs. It was soft and sweet. "William, pumpkin."

"MOMMA!" William exclaimed.

"William, I can't take you, but if you step right there," Peter pointed to the first step, "it will start a chain reaction."

"Chain reaction?" William looked up at Peter, puzzled. As he reached out to grab the railing, a dark figure approached from the other side of Peter.

"So, looks like someone is ready to—" Peter stopped Death in his tracks.

"Death, stay out of this." Peter's eyes held the same glow as the Heart Stone.

"Peter," Death crossed his arms and locked eyes with Peter.

"Death, that boy; all of them deserve their door. They have every right to peace!" Peter stomped his foot, causing blue sparks to flash out.

"Peter, you tapped into the Heart Stone. I am here to open more gateways for you. There are far too many souls for a junior reaper to open. Especially if you're crossing him over." Death pointed to William.

Death took out his scythe, tapped the ground three times, and several sets of stairs appeared. The stairs began to glow and a pixie appeared next to several of the children, attempting to lead them to their own set of stairs.

"Lost boys and girls, Peter Pan's job was to get you here. I commend him for doing that. But now, my pixies are here to take you to your stairs into the thereafter. Please cross over—you have loved ones who have been waiting for you." Death removed his hood, revealing an angelic face and a bright smile.

Before William could step forward, there was an eerie scream as a ten-foot shadow figure came storming out of nowhere to grab William. He was just inches away, when suddenly a long sword came slicing down, pushing the shadow back. Hook was standing before the Shadow, squaring off.

"If you want to touch that boy, you will have to go through me!" Hook gritted his teeth.

William placed his small hand on the rail and took the first two steps.

With each step, the light got brighter. The Shadow's anger flared and it swatted Hook to the side, sending him flying across the courtyard. Hook landed in a heap of rags, leather, and boots, as the Shadow reached out to grab William.

"That soul belongs to me! It was sold to me for power, and I will not be denied what is mine."

"William, come to Momma," came the sweet but urgent voice from the top of the stairs.

William stayed fast to the task of joining his mother. The Shadow reached out to grab him, but the light burned him and he shrieked out in pain. William reached the top of the stairs and giggled, saying just one word, "Momma."

BAG' EM

Dr. Jacobson's hands trembled as he knelt beside the lifeless bodies. The scent of decay mingled with the sterile bite of antiseptic, creating a nauseating blend that clung to the air. Sister Joy stood rigid beside him, her breath shallow, her rosary clutched so tightly that her knuckles turned white.

"Their eyes," she whispered, voice barely audible. "Still open...as if they saw something...something awful."

The call had been made. Knowing the Authorities were on their way, they waited outside. Knowing nothing could prepare them for the horror that awaited them. Children. Lost, forgotten, discarded, like failed experiments.

Dr. Jacobson swallowed hard, forcing himself to remain clinical, though his insides screamed in revolt.

Minutes stretched into eternity before the distant wail of sirens filled the halls. The officers arrived—grim, silent—their gazes dark with the weight of what they'd walked into.

"I can't believe we're getting a call about dead bodies; this is a hospital, is it not? Do you all not understand that sometimes people I don't know die?" one officer said, his voice cold and devoid of humanity.

"Officer." Dr. Jacobson stood up. "Are you a father?"

"What if I am?"

"Let me take you to what we found and then you can judge us. But please let's be mindful, respectful, and most of all, remember these are someone's children." Dr. Jacobson led the officers down the steps.

"What about him?" The officers motioned to Dr. Anderson.

"He will be fine. He is doing far better than those poor souls." Sister Joy clung to her rosary, saying a silent prayer while Dr. Jacobson squatted down to uncover William's body.

Officer Graves was next to speak, his voice as hard as steel. "Who the hell is responsible for this?" he said, looking over the dried-out husk of a child with IV ports still in his body. The officer could see where parts of the child's flesh had been cut way in a meticulous manner.

"The man you just asked about is Dr. Anderson."

Graves' nostrils flared in anger. "Drag his sorry ass down here, Mitch."

Dr. Jacobson rose to his feet, turning toward the entrance as a figure stood there in unnatural stillness. It was Dr. Anderson—smug, arms crossed— his expression unreadable save for the faintest curl of a smirk.

"You can't and won't touch me," Anderson said, his voice laced with a confidence that sent a chill through the room. "I have releases. All legal. Signed by their families. I had every right—"

"Do you think there is one single magistrate that will be okay with you doing this? For what exactly? And all in the name of science and medicine." Graves spat at Dr. Anderson's feet. "There—test that sample. Maybe you can find something in it that will save you."

"Oh, what a naive fool you are, Officer." Anderson chuckled. "Do you think you scare me?"

"Don't be so smug, Dr. Anderson, for the Devil will drag you to Hell one day." Sister Joy shook her rosary fiercely at Dr. Anderson, who rolled his eyes.

"Oh, Sister Joy. If you were not a sister, that passion could be fun." Anderson smirked and gave her a wink, but it quickly faded as Sister Joy brought her foot up, making direct contact with his family jewels, and causing him to double over in pain.

"Are you going to allow her to assault me? I am a healthcare professional; I deserve protection and respect!"

"Sir, I count at least seventy-five bodies here that are mostly intact. Not to mention, five partial bodies, thirty-two jars of preserved parts, and I just looked at the incinerator in the next room. Curious, I pulled out some of the ash and I found teeth."

"I am allowed to burn medical waste you idiots." Dr. Anderson struggled to his feet, glaring at the officers who did nothing to help. "I think it is high time you release me. These idiots have falsely detained me."

"News flash, Mr. Anderson." Graves' words cut like a knife.

"That is Dr. Anderson to you!"

"Doctor nothing. Right now, I am looking at possible mass homicide. I can't imagine how much these poor souls suffered at your hand before they died. Let's face it, I have only seen one adult female body that was next to this young fellow here." Officer Graves pulled back the sheet, revealing a perfectly preserved woman."

"Don't you touch Anna!"

"Oh, so she does have a name. Then that confirms that this is William. Care to explain to me, Doctor, why your late wife and son are here, both dead? If I did not know any better; Anna, is it? looks like she could have died but moments ago, while William looks like beef jerky. Did one of your experiments fail? Why is your wife so well preserved but not your son?"

"That is none of your concern." An evil glint in Dr. Anderson's eye narrowed in on the officer.

Then, a shadow stretched unnaturally along the cold tile floor, slithering toward Anderson like an ink spill moving against gravity. The air in the room thickened, charged with something beyond human understanding.

Graves took a step forward, glaring at Anderson. "You think any kind of legal paperwork can justify—" He paused, his breath hitching. His pupils dilated as his gaze locked onto Anderson's.

A deep, guttural whisper seeped into the room, words ancient and cold. "Failure is not permitted. Broken chains, broken bonds. What was promised was lost. Profits gained; profits lost. Now pay the cost."

Anderson's smirk faltered. His body went rigid as the Shadow coiled around him, creeping up his legs, winding around his torso, sinking into his skin. His breaths turned shallow, strained.

Officer Graves stumbled backward as Anderson's body convulsed, his limbs twisting at unnatural angles, his spine arching so violently that his heels nearly touched the back of his head. The sickening sound of snapping tendons and splintering bone filled the sterile air, louder than the officers' ragged breathing. Dr. Anderson's mouth wrenched open in a silent scream, his lips trembling as though he were drowning in the very shadows now seeping from his flesh.

The mist, thick and tar-like, poured from his chest in writhing tendrils. It pulsed, shifting, coalescing—until faces began to form. Small, fragile faces. Hollow-eyed children, their expressions frozen in eternal agony. Some whimpered. Some sobbed. Others simply stared with a deep, accusatory emptiness that sent ice through the officers' veins.

Graves took a step back, his hand instinctively hovering near his gun— though he knew, in some dark part of his mind, that no bullet could stop what was happening.

Anderson's eyes rolled back, his body still jerking violently, ribs expanding as if something inside him were struggling to burst free. His fingers clawed at his throat, his silent screams turning into a wet, gurgling rattle. His skin turned gray, then ashen, as though the very essence of his being was being siphoned out.

The mist thickened once more, the faces in its depths contorting into grotesque mockeries of life. Then, as if obeying some unseen force, the tendrils snapped back into Anderson's mouth, forcing his jaw wide open in an unnatural, bone-cracking yawn. His cheeks hollowed, his body caving inward. His flesh shrank against his bones, skin peeling, until only a desiccated husk remained—limbs frozen mid-contortion, his body twisted into a horrifying, broken effigy of suffering. A warning.

For a long moment, no one moved. No one breathed. Then, a whisper—high, delicate, childlike.

"Not enough."

The words slithered through the room, barely more than a breath, but it sent a wave of nausea through everyone who heard them.

Sister Joy, hands shaking, pulled a small glass vial from her pocket. She flicked droplets of holy water across the room, whispering Latin prayers under her breath. When the water met the lingering mist, it sizzled, popping and crackling like grease in a hot pan. The shadows recoiled, writhing, before finally dispersing into nothingness.

"Bag him," Graves ordered, though his voice had lost its usual steel. He glanced toward the others, his face pale, his jaw tight. "And for the love of God.. don't leave us alone in here."

No one spoke as they moved to obey.

As the officers turned to leave, after bagging the last body, one of them hesitated at the threshold. His breath caught in his throat.

Somewhere in a dark, distant corner of the room, the soft, eerie giggle of a child echoed—a sound that did not belong.

The room remained deathly silent, save for the lingering echo of a distant drip of condensation against the tile. No one spoke. No one moved.

"Officers, I need to go check on the children in both the wards. This is disturbing, and I don't want what happened here to ever happen again." Dr. Jacobson stepped over Dr. Anderson in his body bag and left Sister Joy to say prayers over all the bodies they'd found.

HEARTS & SKULLS

Time in Neverland passed differently than in the mortal world. Time had not set rules in Neverland. The brief time it took Peter to guide the lost souls to the afterlife, and for the Shadow to lash out in rage, was all the time he needed. Seeing Hook on the ground, reminded him of when he saw the doctor standing over all the children's withered bodies. While he knew they would finally be laid to rest, he was unable to determine Hook's fate.

Peter stepped toward Hook's slumped figure, and the man stirred, shifting to sit up.

Peter slowly said his name. "Hook."

"Yes, Peter. I'm very much still here."

Hook pulled a gold pocket watch from his coat, staring at it for a long moment before pressing the button. A soft click echoed in the clearing, and the lid popped open, revealing an aged photograph. A single tear traced down Hook's cheek before he exhaled a heavy sigh.

"Who is that?" Michael Darling asked as he leaned on Hook to see the watch.

"That would be my son. Well my youngest."

A hush fell over the clearing. The flickering firelight reflected in Peter's wide eyes as he absorbed Hook's words. The Lost Boys murmured among themselves; their usual mischievous energy subdued by the weight of the revelation.

Hook's fingers trembled as he stared at the photo. It was a faded image of a boy, no older than six, laughing with his arms wrapped around a woman with soft curls and bright eyes. His mother. The only woman Hook had ever truly loved.

"I was lucky," he murmured. "Or maybe the shadow just wanted to torment me." He let out a bitter laugh. "One day, I found this sitting in my cabin. A reminder that I had a son I never knew; that cruel fate had played its vile game."

Hook's fingers tightened around the pocket watch, his thumb ghosting over the edges of the boy's chubby cheeks in the photograph. His heart pounded, though he kept his expression carefully guarded.

Their attention was drawn from the depths of Neverland as a blue light flickered, dancing between all of them. Death stepped forward, his skeletal hand gripping Peter's shoulder to still him. Peter struggled under Death's grip, the golden light around them fading as the Heavenly stairs for all the other souls disappeared—all but one.

Peter's eyes darted toward Death. "What's happening?"

Death tapped his scythe against the ground. The blue glowing orb pulsed like a heartbeat, drifting toward the two of them.

"Peter, remember when I warned you about the theft of a soul from a reaper? It is no different with us higher on the chain of command. Peter, this soul was the one of them I had stolen away from the Shadow. I had to break the rules; the very same rules I'm supposed to hold everyone to. But a soul taken from his mother in this manner—I could not stop myself. The only thing I did not count on was the Shadow's hunger."

Death shifted before he explained, his voice as cold as the grave. "I know a balance must be kept, but I did not agree with Nothing's shady deal. I had to hide this soul away. Do you recognize him?"

"The soul from the Heart Stone!" Wendy exclaimed.

Death nodded. "Yes, Miss Darling. That stone held a life force not of its own choice. In doing so, it connected Neverland to the shadows. It allowed the Nothing to latch on to Neverland. Now..."

He gestured toward the boy taking form in the light. "The Beast can once again try to claim him. Because of Hook's contract."

A boy stood before them now, his eyes wide with fear. He looked around, seeing all the unfamiliar faces. Only one face stood out to him, and it was the man in the painting back home.

"Charlie?" Hook whispered, his voice raw.

He wiped a tear from his face. "I've never thought I'd get the chance to see you. I know I should be prepared for hatred, for rejection—I would deserve it. But now, standing before you, my boy. I never realized how heavy the weight of uncertainty would be on my heart. I must say, it's truly suffocating."

Peter stepped between the two of them using his own body as a shield. "No you don't, Hook. You don't get the right to fake it to make it. You had a son all this time and never once did you go looking for him. I don't care if you found out the day you died or thirty years from now, a real father would look for, care for their own."

"If he wants to know me…" Hook said, his voice barely above a whisper.

Charlie stood frozen; his small fingers still clutched in Peter's grasp. His breath came quick and uneven, his wide eyes darting between the man who claimed to be his father, and the boy who he now saw as his protector. The firelight cast jagged shadows across his face, flickering between fear and longing.

A heartbeat of silence, then Charlie swallowed hard and turned to Peter.

"What would you do?" His voice was small uncertain, carrying the tremor of a child standing on the edge of something terrifying.

Peter felt the words like a punch to the gut. His jaw clenched, his hands curling into fist at his sides. A storm churned inside him — anger, envy, something too raw to name. No one had ever given him this choice. His past was an empty void, a wound that festered with every unanswered question. And now, Charlie—this boy who had just become another Lost Boy only moments ago—had been given the very thing Peter had longed for.

His first instinct was to tell Charlie to turn away. To refuse Hook. To let the past stay buried. But then, as his gaze fell on Charlie's frightened face, something inside Peter cracked.

He didn't know what his past had been, but Charlie had a chance now.

And what right did Peter have to take that away?

His throat felt tight as he forced the words out. "I'd want to know."

Hook exhaled sharply, a breath he didn't notice he was holding. Relief flickered in his eyes, but it was chased away by fear. He had spent years haunted by regret, over the son he never knew he had lost. And now, he stood on the precipice of something even more terrifying—that Charlie might listen. What if he learned the truth..and still chose to walk away?

Charlie shifted on his feet, hesitant. He glanced at Peter again, searching his face.

Hook's voice was quiet, unsteady. "I know I don't deserve a second of your time, but if you let me—if you listen—I swear on my life, I'll tell you everything."

There was a long pause. Then, slowly, Charlie nodded.

Hook's breath shuddered, his grip on the pocket watch tightening. He had spent his whole life chasing after things—wealth, power, revenge.

But this? This was the first thing he had ever truly begged for. And now, the truth could either set him free..or damn him forever.

Years ago...

Hook, then a young merchant, stepped off his ship into the bustling port. The scent of salt and spice filled the air as traders called out their wares. But none of it mattered—not when he knew she was waiting.

Caroline stood at the end of the dock, her smile like the first light of dawn. Every time he returned, she was there, her arms open, her laughter wrapping around him like the warmest embrace.

"I thought you'd never come back," she teased, tucking a tiger lily behind her ear. "When the sky turns gray and there's no end in sight…" Caroline bashfully looked up to meet his eyes.

Stopping her with his finger to her lips, he said, "When you're living alone forever."

He leaned in to kiss her. "Your life can seem like a dream. But I'd sail through the fiercest storms to reach you," he vowed, before he allowed their lips to meet.

Months passed in a blur of stolen kisses and whispered promises, but Caroline's father was a businessman, and love alone was not enough.

"A price must be paid for my daughter's hand," the man had said.

Desperation clawed at Hook's soul. That night, as he walked along the moonlit shore, a voice whispered from the darkness.

"When you're walking the streets all alone…there is a place where fortunes are made…for a price."

The Shadow led him to a cave hidden among jagged cliffs. Inside, a parchment and empty bottles lay scattered on the stone floor.

A single sentence was scrawled on the paper:

What will you give to gain what your heart desires?

Hook frowned. "How am I to write? I have no ink. No quill." The shadows shifted, and more words bled onto the parchment. *With blood.*

His breath hitched. He found a shard of broken glass, pressing the sharp edge against his finger. Blood welled, dark and rich, and with a shaking hand, he scrawled a single word:

Anything.

He placed the parchment in a bottle and dropped it into the hollow of the cave wall.

The wind howled.

By morning, fortune found him. Gold filled his pockets, his ship prospered, and Caroline became his bride. They had several children together so he thought he had won.

Until the sea took everything away.

Back in the present, Hook snapped the pocket watch shut. "Words can't express what you mean to me, Charlie." He took a deep breath before letting it out slowly. "When I started to gain wealth, my ship went down in a storm. I never knew your mother was carrying you. It wasn't until years later, when the watch showed up, that I learned the truth."

"That's the watch Mommy gave me," Charlie whispered. "I lost it on the beach."

Hook nodded solemnly. "When the watch reappeared, the Shadow made its price known. Not only my life—but yours. I fought it, feeding it the collected souls of those lost at sea. But now, Peter…watching you set all those other souls free with these stairs…" He gestured to them. "Am I right to assume this is for Charlie?"

Death leaned on his scythe. "Yes. I have been waiting for this soul to cross over."

Charlie's face twisted with anger. "Wait. You locked my soul away for I don't know how long, and now—because of *her*…because of him." He pointed to Wendy and Peter. "I'm finally free, only to be told I have to cross over without even knowing my father?"

A dark mist coiled up from the ground, causing the earth to tremble beneath their feet. A sinister hiss filled the air as the Shadow returned.

"The child's soul was sold to me," the mist snarled. "I have already lost one because this family cannot keep its promises. I will not allow another to escape."

The mist shifted, forming a humanoid figure.

"Please, don't argue," Hook urged. "You have to leave. As your father I am ordering you to go. Now! You aren't safe here." He pushed Charlie toward the stairs. "Charlie..." His voice softened. "Tell your mother how sorry I am. And that I love her."

"Yes, sir." Charlie took a step backward, inching toward the stairs. The Shadow lunged to reclaim its prize, but Hook sprang forward, sword in hand.

"You dare stand against me again? Did you not learn you can't stop me?" the Shadow hissed.

Hook's grip tightened. "That is my son. I love him. You took my life already—why do you need to take his?" He swung his sword, but it sliced only air.

"I did it because I *can*," the Shadow taunted. "Because I *will*. There is nothing you can do to stop me." It reached out, ready to cast Hook aside again—until it suddenly flinched.

A swarm of tiny, glowing creatures buzzed around it, disrupting it form.

"Damn pest," the Shadow spat.

"Caroline!" Hook Called out.

"Tinkerbell!" Peter cried.

Before Peter could reach her, Hook scooped the tiny fairy into his hat, curling protectively around her. The Shadow reformed, striking Hook with an inky tendril, sending him to his knees.

Hook gasped, clutching his chest as dark veins spread across his skin.

The Shadow's poison seeped into him, draining the life from his body.

Charlie screamed, "No! You can't take him!"

Hook forced himself to smile. "It's all right, lad...I made my choice..a long time ago." His fingers trembled as he pressed the pocket watch into Charlie's hands. "Take this...and live."

The Shadow surged forward, but Hook pushed off the ground, using the last of his strength to drive his sword through its core. A guttural cry echoed through the place as the darkness writhed around the blade.

"Go!" Hook roared. "Now!"

Tears streamed down Charlie's face as Peter grabbed his hand, pulling him toward the stairs. "Dad—"

Hook met his gaze, his expression fierce yet full of love. "You were worth it. I'll be all right."

As Charlie vanished into the light, Hook exhaled his last breath. The Shadow gave one final shriek before imploding, threatening to take them both into the abyss, but Death reached out, pulling Hook and Tinkerbell to safety.

Silence fell over Neverland, as a single tiger lily drifted to the ground from atop the golden stairs.

THE WEIGHT OF GOODBYE

With the Shadow defeated, Neverland breathed once more. The island, once shrouded in darkness, hummed with renewal—peace.

The night sky stretched endlessly, its velvety expanse littered with stars that twinkled like scattered diamonds. The trees swayed in a soft, salty-sweet breeze; their emerald leaves no longer twisted by fear. The lagoon, once a dark abyss, glowed with the reflected light of the celestial bodies above.

For the first time in an eternity, Peter wasn't fighting to hold onto something that was slipping away. But even in victory, a new weight settled in his chest. Peter barely noticed the endless eyes on him. He stood with his arms crossed, his jaw tight, watching as Death stepped forward. The reaper's presence no longer chilled the air; no longer sent shivers down their spines. There was only stillness, a quiet acceptance of the inevitable.

Peter turned to Death, his gaze now sharp. "And now what?" he asked. "What happens to them?"

Death, ever calm, ever knowing, simply tilted his head toward the Darlings. "It is time they go home." His voice was a whisper of wind. He gestured to the Darlings. "They do not belong here."

The words struck Peter in the chest, harder than any blade. Peter clenched his jaw, nodding. He turned to Wendy, John, and Michael, who watched him with a mixture of sadness and understanding.

Wendy stepped forward, her expression caught between relief and sorrow. "Peter…" She hesitated, wiping the tears from her reddened eyes. "We can't stay. Neverland isn't meant for us."

He knew this. He had always known. Yet, it didn't stop the ache from settling deep into his bones. Wendy was shown what her life had in store for her. Who was he to deny her a child of her own one day?

"Will you be okay?" John asked, adjusting his glasses as if that would help him make sense of the moment. Able to see the pain written on Peter's face even through his mask.

Peter forced a grin; the same mischievous smirk that once led them into many adventures. "I'm Peter Pan. Of course, I'll be okay." But the words felt empty. His eyes no longer held the sparkle they once had. Peter turned to Death. "What about Tink?" he asked, his voice quiet. "What about Hook?"

Death turned, lifting his scythe in a slow, deliberate motion. The blade gleamed, shifting from shadow to silver as the magic flowed. The moment the metal sliced the air, Hook let out a sharp breath—his body shimmering in golden light, a figure barely visible within the glow.

This went on until finally Hook lay there, with one hand outstretched, holding a flower and his hat in the other hand. A flicker of movement caught Peter's eye. Hook, still breathing, lifted a trembling hand. A single tiger lily rested in his palm, its petals a deep crimson against the roughness of his fingers.

Hook looked to his left as the golden stairs began to fade. "Caroline..." Hook murmured, almost to himself. "I love you."

As the golden stairs flickered, a whisper soft as a lullaby, distant as a dream, echoed back, soft and warm, carrying through the wind like a promise. "Always." As the words faded out of existence, so did the stairs leading to eternal peace.

A shudder ran through Hook's body. He stared at the flower, then at Peter.

"I thought I'd at least end up in oblivion," he muttered, his voice thick with something unreadable. "Didn't think I would ever deserve a set of stairs. But to be here and never truly able to..."

At that moment, a tiny glow fluttered out from beneath Hook's hat—it was Tinkerbell, free at last. Seeing her, Hook let out a breath, as if feeling something he hadn't felt in many years. He recalled the image on his pocket watch, thinking of Caroline's beautiful face then looking at Tinkerbell. "Uncanny," he said.

A hand appeared in front of him. It was Peter's.

"Hook." Peter's voice was gentle. Like that of a friend long forgotten but warm all the same.

"My dear boy." Hook sat still. "I could never thank you enough. You saved my great-grandson. My son. Whatever the Shadow tried to do, it failed. It's all because of you. Thank you."

Hook stared at Peter, wary, and Peter offered his hand again.

"Hook, I am a Lost Boy of Neverland. We may never grow old, we may never die, but we never turn a lost soul away. This is nothing more than an adventure." His expression softened. "Somewhere along the way, you lost your path, but Death saw fit to give you a second chance. If you want it."

Hook hesitated. For a moment, just a moment, something like hope flickered in his weary eyes. And then—a soft flapping, a flickering light— Tinkerbell flew between them.

"Tink," Peter murmured, his heart suddenly heavy. He extended his hand toward her. "Come with me?" She hesitated; for the first time in her long, long existence. Her tiny wings trembled, her eyes flickering with something unreadable. Then, slowly, she turned her gaze—not to Peter, but to Hook.

Death stepped forward, greeting Hook. "Come, let's chat for a while."

"What about Peter? Come my boy. If it were—" Hook was cut short by Death shaking his head.

"I'm sorry but Peter needs to take his friends home now that the Shadow has been sent back to where it came from." Death looked over to Peter, who looked longingly at his friend Tinkerbell.

Tinkerbell fluttered closer to him, pressing a tiny hand to his cheek. "Peter...can I stay this time?" For a moment, he said nothing. Then, he smiled, soft and understanding.

"Of course you can, Tink."

A weight lifted from her shoulders. She twirled in the air before settling on Hook's shoulder, her glow returning brighter than before.

Peter swallowed the lump in his throat. "Take care of her," he said, his voice barely above a whisper.

Hook inclined his head. "I will if only for a little while. And you, boy, take care of yourself. And get those little ones home."

Peter turned to the Darling children and pulled a pinch of pixie dust from his pouch. He sprinkled it over them, his voice lifting into a familiar rhythm. "All right, you know the drill—I want you all to think happy thoughts."

Michael shouted, "Mommy!" Wendy whispered, "Papa."

John straightened his glasses, grinning. "My studies...but of course, Mother and Father."

And just like that, they began to rise, lifted by the weight of their own joy.

Peter took one last look at Neverland before soaring into the sky, leading the Darling children home.

The world was quiet as Peter soared through the night sky, leading the Darling children home. The weight of Neverland still clung to them—the warmth of adventure, the thrill of flight—but the moment their feet touched the ground, reality began to seep back in.

Peter looked through the hospital window and saw them—Mr. and Mrs. Darling. He slipped each of the children in through the oversized window as quiet as a mouse. Michael was the first one in, then John, and last came Wendy. Peter held on to her for a moment longer than her brothers. His heart felt heavy in his chest, almost as if he knew he may never see them again.

"Boy, why are you crying?" Wendy playfully asked.

"I'm not crying. I got something in my eye." Peter fought back his gentle sobs.

"I will never forget you, Peter." Wendy gave him a gentle kiss on the cheek before walking back to her body.

The Darling children looked at Peter one last time, before falling back into their bodies. Peter wasted no time in flying outside as he waved goodbye.

The Darling parents were sat beside their children's beds, their faces pale with exhaustion. Mrs. Darling clutched Michael's tiny hand, her head bowed in silent prayer, while Mr. Darling rubbed slow circles on her back, murmuring reassurances he himself was struggling to believe.

Across the room, Sister Joy stood by the doorway, wringing her hands. A rosery slowly turned in her fingers as she let out a silent prayer.

"Mr. and Mrs. Darling," she whispered, her voice gentle yet uncertain. "I feel the children should be getting better sooner rather than later. Please, just hold on to a little more faith."

Mrs. Darling let out a shaky breath, gripping her husband's hand. "Of course, Sister. I will do anything for my children." Tears trembled at the edge of her lashes, her composure slipping. She turned, burying her face in Mr. Darling's chest.

"I just..I just don't understand. They were so sick. What if—"

"Shh, my love," Mr. Darling soothed holding her tightly. "They will wake up. They must." And then...

A small boy's voice gasped, "Mommy?"

Mrs. Darling's breath hitched. She turned sharply, eyes wide as she watched Michael sit up, rubbing the sleep from his eyes.

"Why are you crying?" he asked innocently, tilting his head. At the same time, Wendy bolted upright.

"Papa!" she cried, throwing herself into her father's arms. He barely had time to react before she wrapped herself around his neck, sobbing into his shoulder.

John blinked awake, fumbling with the sheets. "My glasses—where are my glasses?"

Mrs. Darling let out a broken laugh, reaching for him. "Oh, John, my darling boy..."

The children's eyes swept the room, confusion settling in. Something felt..different. Their bodies no longer ached, and yet—

Michael turned his head frantically. "Where's Peter?"

Silence. Nobody moved. It was as if time itself came to a standstill. Wendy's breath finally hitched. "Michael, hush."

But Michael wasn't deterred. "I wanted to show him to Mommy! He was right here!" He pointed to the corner window that they had just flown in through. Once again, a quiet hush fell over the ward.

"My boy, I think you may have been dreaming," Mr. Darling said sweetly.

From where she stood to the far side of the room, Sister Joy's eyes flickered toward the window. There, on the wall, faint shadows danced along the candlelight, flickering and swaying as if something—someone—was still watching.

She pressed a hand to her heart. "Oh, little one, perhaps you weren't dreaming."

Mrs. Darling frowned. "What do you mean?"

Sister Joy hesitated only for a moment before reaching into the folds of her apron. Slowly, she pulled out a small, worn portrait.

A boy with wild hair and a mischievous grin. Eyes that shone with untamed wonder. She handed it to Mrs. Darling. "Peter Pan," she murmured. "Known by all of us at the orphanage as simply Peter. If you knew him, you were never lonely. He had this spirit about him."

Mrs. Darling's fingers trembled as she brushed over the faded image. "Orphanage?" she whispered. Her brow scrunched up as if trying to see beyond the photograph.

Sister Joy nodded. "Peter passed away some time ago." She smiled softly, though her eyes glistened with unshed tears. "And yet...many have claimed to see him watching over the children. I myself have glimpsed him, just in the corner of my eye. He always seems to know when a child is in need—alerting the doctor, guiding me toward a struggling soul."

She let out a breath, dabbing at the single tear that escaped. "I believe God sends us blessings, every now and then."

The room was silent. Then—"No!" Michael's small voice trembled with raw emotion. He balled his fists in the sheets, shaking his head wildly. "Peter isn't dead! He's a Lost Boy!"

Mrs. Darling turned to him gently, brushing his golden curls back from his face. "Sweetheart, what do you mean Lost Boy?"

Michael's lower lip quivered. "I want to go back," he whispered. "Mommy, I love you but I want to go back. I want my adventure."

Mrs. Darling furrowed her brows. "Back where, darling? What adventure? Sister Joy, please get the doctor."

Michael lifted his eyes, still brimming with childlike wonder. "Back to Neverland."

Peter, feeling a tug at his heart strings, unseen by all, walked over to Michael and whispered into his ear, "Life is the biggest adventure. I will always be with you. Always."

Before he left, he gave the children one final glance and dashed to the window. He flew out of the hospital muttering to himself, "Okay, Peter," wiping a tear from his eye, "second star to the right, straight on till morning. Tink, I hope you're doing okay. When I get back, we will need to talk."

A TEAR FOR NEVERLAND

Peter returned to Neverland, his heart sinking at the sight of the Lost Boys' solemn faces. Their usual mischief and laughter had been replaced with quiet murmurs and downcast eyes. He moved toward them, offering a reassuring smile despite the weight pressing against his own chest. Before he could reach them, a familiar voice called his name.

"Peter. Come."

Death's voice was neither warm nor cold—it simply was. A presence that commanded attention without demand. Peter swallowed hard and turned, making his way toward Death. His steps faltered when he caught sight of Tinkerbell still perched on Hook's shoulder.

The sight stung more than he expected. Tinkerbell had always been by his side, his light in the darkness of Neverland. But now, she sat there, wings fluttering gently, as if she belonged anywhere but with him. The pain in Peter's eyes was evident to everyone.

Still, he forced himself forward, coming to a stop beside Death. He clenched his fists, willing his voice to remain steady.

"Now, Peter, before we say anything—" Death began.

Before another word could be uttered, Tinkerbell suddenly lifted from Hook's shoulder and zipped toward Peter. In a blur of golden light, she landed delicately on the bridge of his nose, pressing a small but firm kiss against his skin.

Peter blinked, startled by the gesture. He could feel the faint warmth left behind, a strange sense of comfort washing over him. "Tink?" His voice wavered with confusion. "What's with the fairy kiss?"

Tinkerbell flew back, hovering in the space between him and Hook.

Her tiny form shimmered with an ethereal glow as she met Peter's gaze. "It is a form of protection," she answered simply.

Peter frowned. Protection? From what? From who? His eyes darted between Tinkerbell, Hook, and Death, suspicion creeping into his chest.

"Why?" he asked, his voice barely above a whisper.

Tinkerbell hesitated, her wings slowing for just a moment. "Because you'll need it."

Silence settled between them, heavier than the humid Neverland air.

Peter's fingers brushed the spot where her lips had touched, a lingering warmth against the growing chill in his bones.

Something was coming.

And Peter wasn't sure he was ready for it.

Death cleared his throat before addressing Peter. "Peter, you are like a son to me, and I know it will be a lot to ask. I need you to continue to share Neverland with Hook. He is, after all, an agent of the afterlife. Now that the Shadow no longer has sway, I am taking James T. Hook under my protection. I will be helping guide him to salvation. One day, it will be the goal to cross him over, but until then, he will need help."

Death took a long pause.

"He needs Tinkerbell, doesn't he?" Peter's words came out flat, but the pain and hurt in them were evident to everyone.

"Only for a little while."

"Why can't you make him a fairy like you did for me?"

"Peter, do you remember how I told you a fairy is made?"

"Kind of. Dust or mist."

"Remember when I reached into my robes and a fine dust came out. How it laughed? That, my boy, is the first laugh of a baby. Every baby born has its fairy. But it appears Tink looks like Caroline because—"

"She comes from her first laugh."

"Yes, Peter. I am sorry. When I reached into my robes, I thought I drew out your mother's laugh, but I was wrong. I first suspected it when Tinkerbell got jealous of Wendy and you. But it was confirmed when Tinkerbell was with Hook on his ship."

"What?" Peter's eyes flew wide open with anger.

"Peter!" Death chastised. "It is not what you think. Even now, the bond between them is not like that of Hook and his Caroline. Tinkerbell is yours, but for now, I need her to be his guiding light. I feel perhaps if he has a constant reminder of his wife, maybe then I can break him of those habits."

"As for me?" Peter asked, standing up tall.

"The kiss she gave you will not only protect you but link you two together. If you are in danger, if you need her, she will be there, Peter. All you need—"

"I know. Faith, trust—"

In unison, Peter and Tinkerbell whispered, "And pixie dust."

Without another word, Peter shot off into the sky, but not before a single tear escaped his eye and fell to the ground.

"Peter!" Tinkerbell called out, but it was too late, Peter was gone.

Peter performed his duties, helping to guide children to the afterlife, but he avoided returning to Neverland as much as he could. Every time he felt Death was near or watching, he bolted. On one such night, Peter came across a father and an older woman looking over the body of a small child.

Peter approached, his heart heavy, and peered down at the young boy.

The child's breathing was labored.

"I don't know how this happened—he just came out of nowhere." The man's voice was shaky as he placed a trembling hand on the boy's.

"Son, where are your folks?" he asked gently.

"I have none. Please, mister...the pain..."

Peter crouched beside the boy, his voice soft and gentle. "Hello, boy."

The child turned his head slightly, looking past the gentleman who had struck him with the car. The old woman gasped. "What is he looking at?" she whispered.

Peter reached out a hand. "Come with me."

The boy hesitated for only a moment before his small fingers curled around Peter's. A weight seemed to lift from his chest, and soon, they were soaring high above the city.

"Where are we going?" the young boy asked, eyes wide with wonder.

"Far away from reality," Peter murmured, gazing down at the sprawling lights below. "I am taking you to a land of make-believe. A home away from home for lost boys like you and me."

As their feet finally touched the ground, the young boy turned to Peter, his wide eyes filled with curiosity. "Who's that?" he asked, pointing to a figure moving gracefully along the trail toward the towering treehouse.

Peter's breath hitched. He couldn't see her face clearly through the soft glow of Neverland's perpetual twilight, but something about her silhouette made his chest tighten. His feet moved on their own accord, stopping just a few steps away from her.

Then, her voice rang out, warm and familiar. "Peter!"

He stiffened, instinctively stepping back as if the sound alone could undo him.

She giggled, a lilting, airy sound. "I won't bite...unless you're into that sort of thing." Her teasing smirk sent a ripple of warmth through him. "Silly boy."

A rush of heat bloomed in Peter's ears, the tips turning a deep crimson red.

"Wendy," he breathed, his voice caught between relief and disbelief.

"What are you doing here? Please—please tell me you didn't..." He couldn't bring himself to say it. His hands clenched at his sides. "You deserve—"

A soft hand pressed against his lips, silencing him.

"I'm far from dead, Peter," Wendy reassured him gently, her eyes filled with knowing tenderness. "Tinkerbell came to me. She said you were in pain... that you needed someone who could help." She frowned slightly. "But I don't see any injury."

Peter swallowed, turning his face away. "Why would you?" The words came out colder than he intended.

Wendy's brows knitted together, but she didn't back away. "Peter, I came all this way because I care about you. Because I'm your friend."

He didn't let her finish.

With a sudden rush, Peter closed the distance, pressing his lips to hers.

A warmth spread through him like the first light of dawn, melting the icy grief that had settled in his bones. For the first time in what felt like eternity, he felt something other than emptiness. When he pulled away, he was met with Wendy's dazed expression, her cheeks flushed a shade deeper than the sunset.

Her breath hitched. "Peter...that's twice now you've stolen a kiss from me."

He grinned, a glimmer of mischief returning to his emerald eyes. "If I were alive, it'd be a lot more than that."

Wendy's lips parted in amused surprise, and she lifted an eyebrow.

"Oh?"

"Yes, Wendy Darling," he said playfully, puffing out his chest. "If I were of the living, I would ask—"

"I know, Peter." Her voice was a whisper, but it carried the weight of something unspoken between them. Her fingers brushed his, and their foreheads touched, a quiet promise lingering in the air. "And I would gladly be that."

A slow clap interrupted their moment.

Peter tensed instantly, turning to see a familiar figure leaning against a tree, his hat tilted at a rakish angle.

"Ah, my dear Wendy," Hook drawled, his smirk softer than usual. "I see you've arrived.. and brought life back into Peter Pan."

Wendy immediately stepped between them; her stance protective. "What do you want, Hook?"

He raised his hands in mock surrender. "Easy, love. I'm one of the good guys now, remember?" His gaze flickered to Peter. "I only came to say goodbye. I have a long-term assignment, and where I must go, Tinkerbell cannot follow." He reached into his coat pocket and withdrew a tiny glowing figure. "I'm giving her back to you, my boy."

Peter blinked, caught off-guard as Tinkerbell flitted into the air, circling him in a shimmering blur of light.

Hook gave a small, knowing smile. "It was Tinkerbell who thought a visit from someone who once touched your young heart might help you heal."

Peter said nothing, his throat too tight with emotion.

Hook tipped his hat. "Take care of yourself, Pan." With that, he turned and disappeared into the shadows of the forest.

Peter barely had time to process before Wendy spoke again, her fingers tracing over his palm as if grounding him.

"Peter, Tinkerbell said I can't stay long."

He exhaled, feeling the soft, tingling sparks dance where their hands met.

"Well, Wendy Darling, I suppose I'd better get you home." He reached into his pouch, letting a cascade of pixie dust spill between his fingers.

"Think happy thoughts," he reminded her with a smile.

Wendy's gaze softened. "Of course." She laced her fingers through his, squeezing gently.

"My happy thought is you, Peter."

And with that, they soared into the sky, leaving only a trail of golden dust behind.

FAITH, TRUST, AND FAREWELL

Peter stood at the window of the Darling home, watching as Wendy, John, and Michael laughed together, the echoes of their childhood games filling the room. It was as if time had rewound, bringing them all back to the nights they had once shared. But even in the midst of their joy, Peter felt the pull of Neverland. He always did.

The stars twinkled in the night sky, calling him home.

"Wendy, it's time. I have to go," Peter finally said, his voice quiet but firm. He turned to her with a small, wistful smile. "But fear not. I will watch over all of you."

Wendy's eyes softened. "Peter, that is so sweet, but you have a job to do."

Peter's grin widened, mischief dancing in his eyes. "You guys are like my family. My Lost Boys... and my Lost Girl."

John smirked. "I suppose that makes me a Lost Man now."

Michael scoffed. "And me?"

Peter laughed. "You'll always be the baby brother, Michael."

With a final glance at the siblings, Peter stepped onto the windowsill, letting the moonlight bathe him in silver. A gust of wind carried him into the sky, back toward the realm where time was never set in stone.

Neverland shimmered beneath him as he descended, the familiar scents of salt and jungle wrapping around him. Tinkerbell was waiting at the edge of the hollow, her tiny arms crossed and a knowing expression on her face.

"Took you long enough," she huffed, wings flickering.

Peter chuckled. "Had to say my goodbyes."

Tink softened, the bell-like chime of her voice gentler this time. "Get some rest, Peter. Tomorrow, we have souls to guide."

He exhaled; exhaustion suddenly heavy on his shoulders. "Yeah..I guess we do."

Time shimmered and bent as days bled into years, yet Peter remained the same. He often found himself visiting Sister Joy at the orphanage, watching as she aged, her hands growing slower, her steps more measured.

But her heart remained as strong as ever.

Dr. Jacobson, once a skeptical man, had set up a small practice within the orphanage's walls. Above his door hung a peculiar sign: *Lost Boys & Girls: Faith, Trust, and a Little Bit of Pixie Dust.*

A gentleman in a finely-tailored coat stopped in front of the door one day, peering at the inscription with a raised brow. "Good sir, you're a medical professional. What is with all this poppycock? Faith, trust, and this rubbish of pixie dust? Have you gone mad?"

Dr. Jacobson only smiled as he leaned back in his chair. "Why, no. Once, not that long ago, a little soul told me that was all it took to get better. And that, my friend, is our goal here."

The orphanage thrived, becoming a place of warmth and hope for children who had lost their way—just as it always had been before the darkness came.

The large clock struck midnight. In the dimly-lit hospital ward, nurses peered warily into the room. "Mrs. Evans, is everything all right?"

Wendy Evans clutched her husband's hand, her grief palpable. "Yes."

One of the nurses hesitated. "I know you're grieving, but we need to take the boy soon. The other nurse mentioned you've chosen a name."

Wendy looked to her husband, who solemnly nodded his blessing. "Yes, we have. His name is Peter Pan Evans."

The nurse smiled gently. "Oh, what a lovely name, Mr. and Mrs. Evans"

"Can I have just a little more time?"

"But of course."

As the nurse exited, Peter stood at the foot of the bed, cradling the spirit of the tiny newborn. The baby's eyes fluttered open, and a giggle, soft as wind chimes, escaped his lips. A golden speck of light floated into the air and split in two. Tinkerbell, ever watchful, darted forward, collecting both fragments and tucking them into a special pouch.

"Seeds for the next generation?" Wendy asked knowingly. Tinkerbell nodded.

"Peter, we need to go," she urged, her chiming voice edged with urgency.

Peter pressed his lips together before snapping his fingers and glancing up the grand staircase that had materialized before him. "Peter, he's but a baby. He cannot climb the stairs. He needs to go to Neverland until Wendy crosses over or a Lost Boy carries him."

"I know the rules, Tink," Peter murmured, his gaze fixed ahead.

"Peter," Tinkerbell warned.

Wendy's voice wavered. "Peter, why won't he go to Neverland? You promised to look after all of us."

Peter stepped forward, placing a gentle fairy kiss on Wendy's forehead. Then, with a bittersweet smile, he walked back to the stairs.

"Peter! Why did you give me a fairy kiss?" she cried. "I know what those are!"

"Because I'm going to cross the little guy over."

Tinkerbell gasped. "Peter, if you cross over, there is no coming back."

Peter cradled the infant closer. "I know. But I have people waiting for me on the other side, and I don't mind looking after him." Gentle tears ran down his cheeks in a constant stream.

Wendy's tears shimmered, as a familiar voice from beyond the staircase called out. "Boy, why are you crying?"

Peter swallowed hard. "Because sometimes, the biggest adventure can be the scariest."

A warm, maternal voice followed. "Oh, my sweet boy, I've been waiting a long time for you."

Sister Agnus appeared at the top of the staircase, extending her hand. "Come now, Peter. Your mother is waiting."

Peter inhaled deeply, then began his ascent. Tinkerbell darted after him, but he turned and shook his head. "No, Tink. This is one adventure you can't join me on. Look after the Lost Boys."

With one last glance at Wendy and Tinkerbell, Peter stepped into the golden light and vanished.

Time continued to move on, everchanging. Wendy sat in her favorite armchair, a fire crackling beside her, the weight of years settling comfortably in her bones. She smoothed the pages of the old book on her lap, her voice steady and warm as she spoke.

"As time moved on, so did we. Michael, John, and I grew up. And when you grow up, you forget the magic of faith, trust, and pixie dust. But Peter... Peter was never forgotten."

She paused, her gaze flickering toward the window where moonlight spilled onto the floor. "Peter came to visit me often in my dreams holding my newborn son. Somehow, that helped me to keep the magic alive. Maybe it was the kiss." She gently brushed her finger where he left his last kiss.

Her husband, reclining in the chair beside her, raised a brow. "Really, dear? You'll brag about another man kissing you?"

She chuckled. "Come now, I was but a child then. Look who I married."

"I know, I know," he muttered, shaking his head with a smile.

"Now, my babes, you know the story of Peter Pan and Neverland."

Wendy closed the book she long ago wrote after her adventures. Where the past and present collided, wrapped in love and memories, and where a silent guardian, who never truly left, fluttered outside the window keeping a watchful eye.

"Remember, all it takes, is faith, trust, and a pinch of pixie dust."

Thank you for reading—I hope you enjoyed the journey.

If you'd like to explore more of my work, see what's coming next, or simply say hello, I'd love to connect with you.

📖 More Books by P. A. Power

- *The Chimera Wolf*
- *The Chimera Clan*
- *Decoding Shady Pines*

Whether you're drawn to shape-shifters, secret societies, or small towns hiding big mysteries, there's another adventure waiting for you.

🌐 Visit my website: www.PA-Power.com

There, you'll find updates on upcoming releases, behind-the-scenes extras, character art, and exclusive content. You can also join my mailing list for early access to new books and subscriber-only bonuses.

Thank you again for your support—it's what makes the next story possible.

See you on the next page,

P. A. Power

www.ingramcontent.com/pod-product-compliance
Lightning Source LLC
Chambersburg PA
CBHW020631250626
47154CB00008B/2626